PICKEREL LAKE 2:
SECRETS REVEALED

Gary Blackburn

Published by

Martin Sisters Publishing, LLC

www. martinsisterspublishing. com

Copyright © 2013 Gary Blackburn

All rights reserved. Published in the United States by
Martin Sisters Publishing, LLC, Kentucky.
ISBN: 978-1-62553-017-2
Fiction/Young Adult/Mystery/Suspense
Printed in the United States of America
Martin Sisters Publishing, LLC

DEDICATION

Dedicated to my wife Ana Teresa ... always encouraging me to keep moving forward and capture my dream.

ACKNOWLEDGEMENTS

A million thanks to my copy editor Kathleen Marusak.

CHAPTER 1

Gusta squeezed the guard's neck a few more seconds and then released him, allowing the limp body to fall to the ground. He checked the man's vital signs, his pulse and his breathing, assuring himself the man was only unconscious and not dead. "Perfect," he thought. The chokehold had worked as planned and the guard was out cold.

He rose and looked to his right, surveying the pathway snaking its way between the building and the first security fence. Everything was quiet except for subdued laughter emanating from inside the prison bunker guard offices. "Security check. Lockdown commencing now." Then that sound, the wrenching reverberation of steel gates banging shut, one-by-one. He stood there shaking, reflecting, and hating all of it. He thought back to his first day in prison, remembering those sounds: the hallway cell block doors; the metal dinner plates scraping against the steel tables; the guard's iron tower gates crashing shut; and then the final clanging of the individual cell block doors, closing in rapid succession like a giant Gatling gun firing into the night blackness; the omnipresent, grating, metallic noises. How he despised them all! But soon, this nightmare would be over.

He turned and edged slowly, noiselessly, down the narrow pathway, hugging the perimeter wall of the prison compound. Reaching inside his jacket, he checked the knotted bed-sheet coiled against his body. Continuing to inch forward, he reviewed the plan over and over in his mind. It should work. It had to work. He knew the guards at the north tower took a short break around midnight, after lockdown, and that would provide his opportunity to escape.

"Cell block eleven lockdown: units one, two, three and four secure. Kill the night light, Jackson. Follow your bud, Gusta's, example. Loser already asleep."

Gusta smiled to himself, remembering those first several weeks in prison when he was assigned to repair inmate clothing in the tailor shop. All those mannequins. He kept staring at them as they hovered around him and the other prisoners. There had to be another use for them, more than just modeling clothes to be sewn and repaired. And then it hit him. It was simple, really. One day at work, when everyone else was on break, he took one of the mannequins, snapped off its head, stuck the head into an oversized pocket inside his bulky jacket and jammed the headless body into an unused, back storage closet. The next day, after pocketing a tube of brown paint from the art class, he was good to go. Tonight that head, painted brown to match his own hair color, rested on top of his bunk, wedged between the pillows and the blanket, facing his cell wall. From a distance, the cellblock guard performing the final lockdown count would assume it was him, Gusta, trying to get some early zees.

As Gusta stopped to listen for the final lockdown verifications, he heard the faint, muffled command to report the prisoner count. Then, the inside compound lights were dimmed to security level, and it was nearly silent. His plan was working perfectly.

Continuing to edge down the narrow walkway towards the north tower structure that loomed high into the night sky, Gusta pushed himself flat against the compound wall and froze, as he heard subdued voices inside the compound in front of him. Holding his breath as he waited for the silence to return, he remembered other voices, those from the day he arrived at this hellhole several months earlier.

"Get up against the damn wall and shut up. Where the hell you punks think you are? This is a prison, not a schoolyard." The captain of the guard walked around the small group of new inmates, continuing to shout instructions laced with obscenities, twirling his nightstick baton in his hands. Then he stopped at the side of a selected target next to Gusta and slammed the edge of the baton into the legs of the inmate, demanding he stand at attention. Immediately, everyone stood more rigid.

Except for the memory of an older, skinny boy approaching him in the yard after the check-in process, the rest of that first day blurred in his mind. Gusta was sitting on a metal bench in the prison yard, watching a basketball game, when the boy walked over and sat down.

"Hey, man, name's Dougie. What's yours? What you in for?" He reached over to shake Gusta's hand.

"Yeah, it's Gusta. I don't know why I'm even here. Been some kind of stupid mistake. Only seventeen and I should have gone to a minimum security place instead of this hellhole."

"I know, I know. That's what everyone says. They don't belong here. Listen, it's enlightenment time for you, seein' yur a new fish. And believe me; I know what I'm talking 'bout. I've seen the worst, having been here for over five years. Anyway, some friendly advice, the most important, keep your antennae turned on, and that means watch your back, 'specially during shower time. The big dogs, the mothers who think they are in charge here, are always on the prowl for new meat, and you will be mighty tempting. They'll be climbing all over themselves for a chance to be the first to plug your cherry. You get what I'm talking about here?"

Gusta looked into Dougie's contorted face with red tangled hair hanging over his forehead, noted his watery eyes and crooked smile sporting broken front teeth, and smelled his halitosis-laced breath.

"I hear you. I hear you. Don't worry; I can take care of myself."

"Yeah, yeah, I know. Yur a big, strong guy and all but believe me, these animals attack like wolves in packs, and then they throw dice to see who wins first place, second and third. Ya know? Anyway, just think of me as your first friend in the joint here. Ya'll need all the friends you can get. I head up the gang called the 'In Crowd' and I also handle most of the trading business, if you have money for cigs, chocolate bars, jerk-off mags, you know, all that shit. So, here's your first gift, on the house. Don't have to pay me nothing. Just remember me when you need something from the outside." Dougie handed Gusta a small, hand-carved wooden cross.

"What's this, man? I'm not religious. Don't need this crap."

"Hold on, virgin white boy. Don't go losing your panties. Let me show you something important." Dougie glanced around at the yard, bent down over the wooden cross and pulled it apart, exposing a four-inch metal blade, and then quickly reinserted it back into the wooden shaft of the cross.

"What the hell is that?" exclaimed Gusta.

"For your protection, keep this cross with you at all times. It's small enough to fit in your prison pockets. And, if they search you, just pull it out and say some Hail Mary prayers, or whatever. Looky here. You press this small button on the end of the wooden piece or it won't open. Guards too stupid to open it will think it's just your prayer cross. But keep it with you for your defense, especially the first few days you're in this screwed-up place. For sure, some of the guys will test you, but once a few weeks go by, they'll leave you alone."

Dougie hesitated and nervously glanced around.

"I know what the hell I'm talking about, personal experience and all. You could say I learned the hard-ass way. Know what I mean? And you can join our gang for extra protection. We got some big, ugly, mean sons-a-bitches with us that you'll need on your side."

"Thanks, I guess," said Gusta. He took the small wooden cross and slipped it into his oversized pants pockets. And for the first time since arriving at the prison, he felt real fear creep over him.

"Well, got to go, my man. But about this gift. It's not a charity thing. You do understand that, right, my white friend? You need a gang to survive in this place. And remember to trade with me for your necessities and shit. I understand from Charlie, the check-in guy, you got a few bucks in your prison savings account. Spend it with me on trades and join our gang, and we'll be square. You good with that?"

Dougie stood up and punched out his fist to signal his departure. Half-smiling, Gusta returned the clenched fist and watched his new friend turn and walk away. When he reached into his pocket and touched the small wooden cross again, he felt a little more secure, but still wondered how he would survive.

A few days later, when Gusta had gone to the laundry room to wash some dirty clothes, he heard a commotion in the back corner, near the dryers.

"Well, Ralphie, time to welcome you into the fold and go through the initiation process. Frank, grab hold of his arms and help me hold him down. Little white ass, you're gonna love this experience."

"Come on, guys. Never did nothing to you. Let me up. Help me, guards, help!"

"Yell all you want, Ralphie. Guards are at dinner break, and nobody gonna hear you with these machines clanking away. Hold him, Frank, while I turn the little bitch over and pull down his drawers."

Gusta had walked around the corner just in time to see the two burly inmates holding Ralphie in place and stripping away his clothing. While the one named Frank held the victim's arms and head, secured inside his pulled-down shirt, the other attacker slammed a chair under the young inmate and spread his legs. The boy screamed that he would pay them money, anything to stop. But the two attackers just laughed as they prepared to indulge themselves.

To everyone's surprise, Gusta raced to the man positioned nearest the young boy and, without a word, threw a solid punch behind the attacker's right ear. The man fell to the ground, screaming obscenities. Frank released the boy and lunged at

Gusta, catching him off-balance and falling with him to the concrete floor. As they struggled to get up, the first attacker recovered from Gusta's punch and jumped into the melee. Now the two men began to pummel Gusta with punches. The young inmate grabbed his clothing and ran screaming from the room.

Then Gusta remembered the cross. He managed to break free, stood up and pulled the wooden cross from his pocket. He held it up to the attackers and pressed the secret button.

"Now look at that, Frank. Mr. Hero here is going to pray to Mary or Jesus to help him create a miracle and save his white virgin ass. It ain't gonna happen, new fish. We're gonna beat the crap out of you and then use up a whole jar of Vaseline, since you volunteered to take our young boy's place." The attackers moved in.

Gusta pulled the cross apart and held the knife blade in front of him while the two men momentarily hesitated. When the main attacker lunged forward, Gusta summoned up his animal trapping experience, dodged the aggressor, and sliced his arm with the knife. The attacker groaned in pain, grabbed his bleeding arm and fell to the floor. Then Gusta advanced on Frank, whose eyes filled with terror.

"You got ten seconds to get the hell out of here, or the next cut will be to separate you from your balls," said Gusta as he menacingly lunged forward, ready to plunge the knife into the man's gut.

"OK, asshole, we're out of here. But this ain't over, hero boy, not by a long shot."

"We'll see what Dougie and the In Crowd gang have to say about that," Gusta returned.

Gusta stood poised with the knife while Frank helped his wounded friend stand up and together, they departed, slowly backing out of the laundry room, spouting threats. It was over and Gusta had won his first small victory. After that, word got around fast not to mess with the new guy, Gusta, because of his association with the In Crowd and his special wooden cross.

Gusta smiled at the memory.

Then he looked at his watch and saw it was almost midnight. The north tower guards would soon be taking their break. Just a few more minutes. Time to move on and get the hell out of this place.

"Hey, Jack, come on. Let's go down to the mess hall and grab some mid-rats."

Gusta heard the two guards descend the metal stairway, pass through the doorway leading into the tower, cut across the path in front of him, and go down another stairway to the lower courtyard and the mess hall. They would be gone at least thirty minutes. It was quiet in the compound once again.

He glanced up at the tower, watching the rotating searchlight slowly illuminate each section of the grassy yard area beyond the first security fence. It took about thirty seconds to complete each sweep. The spot where Gusta crouched was dimly lit, allowing him to easily scale the perimeter fence and not be seen. He waited for the perfect moment.

Now! The spotlight had made its sweep and was beginning its return journey away from his location. Gusta pulled out the knotted sheet from inside his jacket, uncoiled it, and threw it over the security fence, entangling part of the coil on the barbwire covering the top of the fence. He tugged on the coiled sheet, embedding it into the barbwire, and pulled himself up, hand-over-hand, to the top and then shimmied down the other side. He snapped the coiled bed sheet loose from the barbwire, gathered it together and ran over to the side of the north tower, flattening his body against the tower wall as the rotating search light returned. His breath came out in heavy, nervous gasps when he felt the cold, damp stones of the tower against his back. Perfect timing. He waited for another rotation of the tower searchlight. Now the dangerous part of his plan would be tested.

The searchlight returned and again began to rotate away from him. Gusta burst across the dimly lit open field to the second perimeter fence, threw his knotted bed sheet on top of the outside fence, and pulled himself up and over, landing on the ground exhausted. The searchlight rotated around again to his location. No time to snap off and reel in the bed sheet. He lay flat on the ground, breathing into the moist leaves with mud against his face, and waited, watching as the searchlight swept past his location, illuminating the coiled bed sheet hanging on the fence. He considered praying that it would not be seen…almost, but refrained since he didn't believe in prayer. Instead, he reached into his pocket and held onto the wooden cross. He listened for an alarm to sound. Nothing. He thought to himself how lucky he was that this prison had neither motion sensors installed nor dogs patrolling the area between the perimeter fences.

When the searchlight swept past him, Gusta jumped up, snapped off the bed-sheet coil from the fence, bundled it all together and ran into the forest surrounding the prison facility. Once inside the protective trees and shrubbery, he turned to face the prison building one more time and shook a clenched fist in the air.

"Three months in this hellhole, and it's over. I ain't never going back. Pa will let me hide out in one of his root cellars. I can trap and shoot my own food. I'll be fine. And Justin and Sheriff Cooper...be prepared, shitheads. Revenge is on its way."

He turned and ran deep into the woods, smiling to himself, tasting the wind of newfound freedom against his face.

CHAPTER 2

"Justin, hurry up. The bus will be here any minute." Christy smiled at me with pancake syrup running down one corner of her mouth.

"Patience, little prissy missy. We have thirty minutes and besides, the bus is always late. You know Art takes his sweet ol' time, 'specially after a snow storm like we had last night."

"Justin, are we still allowed to sing that song about Art?"

"Which song, Christy?" I knew what she was talking about. I wanted her to sing it at the breakfast table. It would be a hoot. I smiled to myself and gave my cute little sister the go-ahead nod.

"I know how it goes," she giggled. "Art, Art, let a fart and blew his pants clean apart." Her bubbling laughter echoed over the breakfast table and through the kitchen area. I stole a quick look at Gramps who, upon hearing the song, choked on his cup of coffee and spit part of it out onto the table in front of him.

"Now children, it's not nice to make fun of Mr. Hagen," Gram said. "He has been faithfully driving that school bus for…. My, how many years now? I think over twenty-five years and never had an accident. He takes good care of all you rowdy kids." She added a couple more pancakes to the stack on the plate next to me, sat down, touched Christy's nose with her finger, and reminded her to be nice.

Gramps was recovering from the coffee choking spell and wiping his chin with the back of his shirt sleeve.

"You younguns got so much time on your hands to make jokes about people; take some of that extra energy and haul a load of firewood into the basement storage cellar before you head off to school." He scowled at me while brushing his thinning hair away from his deeply wrinkled, flax-colored face.

"But I haven't finished my breakfast yet," I protested.

"No matter, we're out of wood, and it will be extra cold today with last night's snowfall and all. You got plenty of time before the bus gets here. Haul yourself outside, load up your sled, one load be plenty…take maybe fifteen minutes." He took a long drag on his cigarette, punctuating his final instruction with a raspy coughing spell.

"I want to help! I want to help!" Christy was jumping up and down in her chair, her blond ringlets bouncing around her cherub, pearly-skinned face.

I started wolfing down the rest of my breakfast and stole a glance at Gram for her go-ahead. Christy had hold of my shirtsleeve, pleading to go along on the wood- hauling adventure.

"If you could get a small load, it would be nice. Dad's not feeling well today. I'll have your lunches packed for you, ready to go, and will put in an extra blueberry muffin," Grams said. She smiled at me with that unique substitute mom's look, her short black, grey-streaked hair curling down over her aged, yet youthful-looking face.

For Grams, I would do anything. Gramps could stick the wood pile up his butt. I stood up from the table, gobbled down one more bite of pancake and finished off my orange juice.

"Come on, Christy. Let's go. We need to make this quick."

"Hooray! I get to help. I get to help," Christy exclaimed. I was continually amazed by the unbridled enthusiasm of my sister. She jumped up from the table and followed me over to the door of the kitchen that led to the mudroom. We pulled on our snow boots and wrapped ourselves in heavy jackets, earmuffs and gloves. I glanced at the outside thermometer gauge and read fifteen degrees below zero. For the middle of November, that was super frigid. At least there was no wind blowing to drive the temperature lower.

I closed the door leading back into the kitchen while Gramps yelled some final instructions to me.

"Be sure and get a mix of dry kindling and some green birch logs. Last time you only loaded up the small dry crap. Pay attention to what you're doing," he bellowed.

"Yes sir, yes, captain, sir. I got Christy here to instruct me," I shouted back, closing the mud- room door to the kitchen. I heard Gramps mutter something about a smart mouth to Gram. Christy giggled again as we pushed open the outside door and stepped out into a very cold, white winter wonderland.

The air was pure and clean, and our breath billowed out like balls of soft cotton. The sky was a deep, rich blue color with no clouds in sight. The dark green pine trees surrounding the lakeshore stood out in sharp contrast to the brilliant white snow covering the tree branches and the ground. And it was so peaceful. I never tired of being outside on these enrapturing Minnesota mornings following a snowstorm.

As we slogged our way towards the storage shed, crunching the snow under our boots, Christy filled me in with detail about her new teacher. She said her previous one was pregnant and had to quit teaching for a couple months.

When we reached the shed, I opened the door and pulled out my, long cherry-red Ryder sled, a present from Santa Claus last Christmas. I closed the door, set the sled on the snowy ground and knew what was coming next.

"Give me a ride, Justin, give me a ride!"

"OK. Hop on top of the sled. Only a short one to the wood pile." I helped her sit atop of the wooden slats, placed her feet in the gaps by the steering handles, and told her to grab the side rails. I went to the front of the sled and began pulling on the rope, gliding the red Ryder toward the tarp-covered woodpile next to the back cabin road, thankful it was just a short distance. My sister was getting bigger and heavier, and soon she would be too old for our special sled times together.

"Jingle bells, jingle bells, jingle all the way," she sang as I pulled the sled up to the woodpile.

Wow! Would Christmas really be here in just a little over a month?

"All right, little big sister. Help me load up the sled." I untied a corner of the cover tarp, and together we piled on small pieces of dry kindling. Then we added larger cuts of birch and pine logs. When we finished, I secured the tarp cover over the mountain-size stack of wood. There was enough to last all winter long. Then I grabbed the rope and started to pull the sled back to the house.

"Hang on to the side of the load, Christy. Make sure it doesn't roll off." She did her best to balance our stack of wood, and I carefully pulled our bounty to the entrance of the basement cellar. When we were close to the sides of the cellar doors, I stopped. I reached down and flipped both doors open, exposing concrete steps leading down to the entry door of the basement. Looking down, I realized Gramps was right. We were almost out of wood! And today, Grams would need to keep the old wood furnace burning to warm our ancient, drafty house.

"OK, help me throw the wood down into the cellar storage. Grams will need lots of wood today." We grabbed the green logs first and then the kindling, and tossed them down into the cellar storage hole. The logs made a clanking sound, like bowling pins being knocked over, as they bounced down the concrete steps and slammed into the metal basement door. Laughing with every throw, Christy thoroughly enjoyed this part of the job. Soon, we were finished, and I pulled the two doors shut, making a loud banging noise that echoed into the crisp morning air.

"Go back inside and get our lunches together while I put the sled back. School bus will be here any minute." She ran up to the mudroom door and into the house while I took the sled to the storage shed. I took off one of my gloves and touched the end of my nose, realizing it was cold, numb and had no sensation of feeling to it. Man, it was cold outside. Needed to get inside and warm up a little before waiting out by the road for the bus.

"Thank you, my dears, for bringing in the wood," Grams said as she smiled at us. "Your lunches are ready. Grab your backpacks. The bus will be here any minute." She reached down to give Christy a hug and kiss.

Sweet Grams…always our loving angel.

"Bye, Gram, bye, Gramps," Christy yelled as we went out the front door.

Grams waved back at us while Gramps grunted some sound with his face buried in the "Park Rapids Enterprise" newspaper.

Going out the front door, I glanced back at the newspaper and noted the headline: 'Local Youth Escapes from Prison.' *I need to take a look at the newspaper tonight after school,* I thought. Then thinking about it prompted a foreboding shiver to vibrate through my chilled body.

CHAPTER 3

"Man, it's freezing out here." The wind had picked up and was swirling snow everywhere, chilling us to the bone. Christy looked up at me, still smiling, though her teeth were chattering. Then we heard the familiar grinding sounds of the transmission on the school bus, downshifting gears at the top of the hill, lumbering down the icy highway toward us. Christy got excited and started waving at the bus. It finally swerved to a stop at the side of the road. Art punched open the folding bus doors, and none too soon, we clambered on board, kicking the compacted snow off our boots.

Art grunted some kind of greeting as we moved towards the middle of the bus, searching for our friends. Christy slid into a seat next to a couple of her giggly girlfriends, and I found a seat near the back, next to my friend, nicknamed Charlie Horse. He was in my grade, an okay guy, kind of slow mentally and physically, but always friendly and easygoing. We greeted one another, and then he started describing his latest ice fishing experience with his dad up at the south end of Pickerel Lake. Asking a few questions, I listened to him, envious that he had a dad to take him on ice fishing excursions. I only had Gramps and was forced to endure his chain smoking, sleeping, snoring and farting while I did most of the work. And, since our stash of frozen fish was getting low, Gramps and I would have to make a trip to the ice house in the next couple of days.

With Art using creative downshifting techniques and grinding the gears to prevent the wheels from spinning on the new snow, the bus groaned up a steep hill. The snowplows were late today, and I had to admit, for an old geezer, Art was indeed still a professional at his job.

Finally, we pulled into the parking lot of Dorset Elementary School and Christy and all her friends noisily exited the bus. When she turned and waved good-bye to me, I mouthed back to her to have a fun day at school. Wasting little time, Art started the bus back up, and eased out of the school parking lot onto the highway towards Park Rapids Junior High.

After another fifteen minutes, Art maneuvered the bus into the designated drop-off zone, and Charlie and I stood up with all the other noisy kids to exit. I glanced out the window and spotted cousins Robyn and Marlene waiting near the front steps of the school building. Right on! It was great seeing them again.

I jumped off the bottom steps of the bus, adjusted my glasses and backpack, and jogged over to greet them.

"Well, Mr. Detective guy, about time you got here." Robyn gave me a quick hug as Marlene hung back, just waving at me. We crowded up the front steps with all the other students, comparing the experiences of our weekend while the school bell clanged out its warning to check into our homeroom. Halfway down the hallway, Robyn pulled me aside, around the corner of the first set of lockers, and whispered she had some good news. She pulled out an envelope and handed it to me. It was addressed to Robyn with only a return name printed, 'Audrey,' but no street address and postmarked, Duluth, Minnesota. My hands were shaking as I stared down at the envelope and then looked back at Robyn.

"Go ahead, silly, open it. There is a note 'specially for you,'" Robyn said. We pressed up against the lockers, forming a circle, ignoring the mass of students heading to their lockers or to their homerooms. I opened the letter marked Justin and decided to read it out loud as Robyn and Marlene tilted their heads to listen.

Dearest Justin,

Sorry I took so long getting back to you. I miss you and the Pickerel Lake gang so very much. You cannot imagine how many nights I cried myself to sleep after we first moved out here.

We are settled into our new location here in Duluth. I can't tell you our exact address yet. Dad says there continues to be some secret government stuff he needs to take care of before we can divulge our new location. But he promised me it will be soon…possibly a couple weeks.

How are you doing? Are you enjoying your first experience at Park Rapids Junior High? How I miss not being there with you, and Robyn and Marlene. I was so looking forward to this school year with all you guys. Now I am in a strange new school with very few friends and it has been difficult.

Justin, say hello to Eric for me next time you see him. I hope you two are not still playing dangerous detective games over Randy's death. I heard Gusta was sentenced to three years in the juvenile detention center in Appleton. Guess you don't have to worry about him for awhile. And one more thing,

Justin, keep this secret: Dad says his department is going back to Pickerel Lake this next spring to capture that giant fish out there. Or are there really two monster fish?

I have to sign off for now. I promised Dad not to say too much. I miss you every day. The memories of this past summer and those precious few weeks all of us spent together and knowing Randy before his untimely death will remain in my heart forever. Remember me. Remember us. My feelings for you remain unchanged.

All my love, Audrey.

I turned my head to wipe away a couple tears, then folded Audrey's letter and put it in my pocket. For a few brief seconds, my mind flashed back to last summer when Eric and I were searching for the monster fish in Pickerel Lake before our cousin Randy was murdered.

When Audrey had to move away for security reasons related to her dad's job, I felt as if my life had come to an end. Was there hope for us now? I handed the envelope back to Robyn. She took it and reached out her hand, gently touching my face.

"She wrote us a letter inside the same envelope. It was similar to what she told you, except you got all the mushy stuff. Stay positive, Justin. Audrey said she may be able to come back and visit us soon."

The second bell began clanging, the sound reverberating up and down the hallway.

"Hey, we need to get to our homerooms," exclaimed Marlene. "See you at lunch, Justin." Robyn squeezed my hand as both cousins turned and walked quickly down the hall to their homeroom. I waved to them and went over to my locker, opened it, jammed in my jacket, pulled out my classroom books and slammed it shut again.

"Well, hello, farm boy. How's it hanging?" Some ninth grade jerks passed by and pushed me into my closed locker door, laughing, then swaggered down the hall to their homeroom.

Yes, it's going to be another day in paradise, I thought to myself. *Screw it. Have to deal with it.* I reached into my pocket and felt Audrey's letter, remembering her comment about playing detective. Eric was going to call tonight and detail the plan to meet in the Cities to check out the Nickelson brothers and their strip club downtown. He said he had inside information about evidence at their club that would definitely link them to Randy's murder. Sorry, Audrey, the detective work had to continue, for Randy's sake. I smiled to myself, thinking about my first love, Audrey; my best friend, Eric; and my cousins, Robyn and Marlene. I knew we all would soon be together again, working on the case.

CHAPTER 4

"Stop daydreaming, son, and help me carry our gear out to the truck. Time's a wasting and the fish are gettin' hungry." Gramps held the back porch door open and I pushed my way past him, struggling with a couple decoy poles, a large fish net and two spears. He followed me out the door with the food cooler and the two blankets. We threw the supplies into the back of our old Chevy pickup and climbed inside the front seat. He struggled with starting up the straight six-engine, pulling on the choke lever and stomping on the accelerator. The engine gasped against the cold morning air. When it finally caught, he gunned it a few times, jammed the truck into first gear and chugged down the side cabin road onto the frozen lake.

It was a crisp, clear, cold Saturday morning and today I actually looked forward to this trip with ol" Gramps. Not my favorite fishing pal on these excursions, but I had to admit he knew a lot of secrets in spearing any northern pike that might venture past the water hole inside our ice-fishing house.

I glanced out the window, watching the pine-clustered shoreline glide by our moving truck. This was always a unique sensation, driving on top of the frozen ice-covered lake. I'd had nightmares in the past, dreaming our car suddenly crashed through the top of the ice cover, sinking down through the cold, murky water, floating to the bottom of the lake where we remained trapped inside the car, unable to unlock the doors and escape. Several nights ago, I woke up screaming for someone to get us out of the watery grave. Of course, I realized now, that was crazy nonsense. It had been a frigid November and the ice on this part of the lake was at least a foot thick...enough to support a semi-truck.

I focused back on the present, looked out the front window and saw our little green-painted ice fishing shed coming into view. It was sitting in quiet solitude at the narrows location, which connected the two sections of Pickerel Lake.

Gramps pulled up next to the shed, the tires making a crunching sound on top of the snow-covered lake, grinding our pickup to a stop. He barked out some order to me about grabbing the supplies from the pickup bed while he stomped out of the truck, slammed his door shut and walked over to the shed door, unlocked it and pushed inside. I followed close behind, my arms loaded with our gear.

It was dark inside our square, eight-by-eight-foot enclosure, until he struck a match and lit our kerosene lamp that was sitting on a small, makeshift wooden table. I lay the spears with the other gear on the floor of the shed, which was the ice surface of the lake, and turned around to go back and get the cooler and blankets. The wind was picking up and in spite of the bright morning sun glaring on the snow-covered lake surface, the outside temperature gauge read seven degrees below zero.

I took the remaining supplies from the pickup and rushed back inside our temporary home. I put the cooler and blanket on top of my bench and sat down, watching Gramps stuff the old Ben Franklin pot-belly stove with crumpled-up newspaper, dry twigs and a couple birch logs. He lit the newspaper, which ignited the twigs, closed the pot-belly stove door and we soon had a roaring fire. Our little heater started to warm up our frigid ice fishing shed.

"Hand me that eagle hook spear and I'll break up the surface ice on our fishing hole." He took the long spear from my hand and poked it into the ice-covered surface fishing hole again and again, until the surface ice was broken apart. Because our shed kept the lake surface temperature warmer here, the ice was only about eight inches thick with a thin frozen film over the ice hole. He reached for a large strainer spoon from the corner of the shed and scooped up the loose ice chunks from the hole and tossed them aside. Leaning the spear back against the wall of the shed, he sat down on his bench across from me and released a sigh. Reaching into our cooler, he pulled out a thermos bottle and poured two cups of hot, steaming coffee into individual cups and handed one to me.

"Well, Justin, this is going to be a good day...we'll spear several fish. I can feel it in my bones. We'll give it a few minutes to warm up and then you can set our decoy lure into the ice hole."

I nodded my head in agreement, sipped at the hot, black coffee and stared down into the blue-green ice hole. Even though the carved-out area was only about twenty- two inches in diameter, because our ice shed sat in the narrows location where the water depth is only about seven feet, ample sunlight shone through the ice-covered lake surface, reflecting off the

31

silt lake bottom, and up into the shaft of the ice hole, creating an eerie, shimmering iridescent glow to the water. I leaned over and stared into the green-colored abyss, able to see a faint reflection of my face on top of the water's surface. Through the crystal-clear water, I could see down to the silt-covered bottom of the lake and spotted dozens of large, hungry northern pike, swimming near our ice hole, searching for their next meal.

"OK, son, it's toasty in here. Set up the decoy lure and we'll see if we attract any takers." He lit up a cigarette and sipped on his steaming coffee.

I pulled off my gloves, reached down into our pile of supplies and set my spear with its attached rope in my corner of our ice shed. I next retrieved the small rod with the attached line and decoy lure. Man, that decoy was a beaut. It looked just like a three-inch chub minnow with red and white stripes racing over its shimmering grey-scaled body. There was a thin, flexible rubber tailfin that, when the decoy dangled in the water, waved back and forth, ever so slightly, moved by the lake currents. I set the pole onto the V-shaped support device driven into the ice, next to the fishing hole.

Untangling about four feet of line from the tip of the pole hanging over the ice hole, I lowered our decoy lure into the murky, blue-green water. It reached about a foot below the bottom of the ice hole and as I peered down to take a look, I could see it dangling, moving back and forth with the current. The sunlight pierced the lake's ice cover, reflected up from the bottom of the lake, and perfectly illuminated our stripe-covered faux minnow body. Gramps bent over to take a look into the hole just as an extra strong lake current caught the lure, causing the tail fin to wiggle slightly, creating an almost life-like appearance and swimming action to our little fake minnow.

"You did a right good job. We can see the decoy and so can all our fish friends. It won't be long, a northern will poke his head into that space to check out our minnow and Momma will have fresh fish for dinner tonight. Get your spear ready. I'll take the first one and you'll get the next."

I glanced at my spear, leaning in the corner behind me, feeling a little trepidation since I had only speared one fish in all my life, last winter when I went out with Gramps. I watched him pick up his longer, almost harpoon-like spear, leaving about six feet of rope coiled on the ice floor, next to the fishing hole. Then, wrapping the extra rope in a circular fashion around his left hand and elbow, he moved to the edge of his bench, positioned his right hand onto the middle of the spear, and rested the five-pointed tip on the ice.

It got awfully quiet inside our ice shed except for the pot-belly stove emitting sounds of crumbling, burning wood and the outside wind whistling through the cracks in the walls of our ten-year-old, in-need-of repair, ice-fishing house.

Then we saw it. A medium-sized northern pike inched his nose up to the decoy lure and stopped about three inches away. You could almost hear the wheels turning in that tiny fish brain: "What is this? Lunch or some weird minnow I've never tasted before."

We watched it back up and start to swim past the decoy, through the middle of our ice hole, deciding to pass on lunch. Fatal mistake. Gramps had already stood up, arched the spear over his head and now thrust it into the open fishing hole. A direct hit. The razor-sharp ice spear tongs ripped through the glistening surface, continuing through the water and into the mid-section of the northern pike, spilling a stream of red blood into the lake. The pike made a quick lunge, attempting to swim away from the ice hole, but Gramps was too fast for him. He pulled back on the attached spear rope, reeling the fish up through the ice hole and slamming the pike body onto the icy floor of our shed, and finally placed his snow boot on top of its head and gill area. The fish struggled briefly with a few more flops and then lay still.

"Wow, Gramps! That was fantastic. He's at least a seven-, eight-pounder."

"It weren't nothing, son...you could've done the same. Hand me that fish storage bucket behind you." I handed him the bucket. He jerked the spear blades out of the bloodied fish, picked it up and dropped it into our bucket. He placed his spear back in the corner of our shed and sat down. "Now it's your turn."

I gulped, beginning to feel nervous. I remembered the trouble I had last year spearing one little three-pounder on our last ice fishing excursion. But Gramps was right. I could do this. *Buck up, Justin. Buck up.*

"Let's eat one of momma's sandwiches before you try for the next one." He reached down into the cooler and handed me one of the bologna and cheese sandwiches and a Shasta Cola. I began eating my lunch and looked over at Gramps with admiration for him, at least for this particular moment. Most of the time, he was a very difficult, demanding person to live with, but now I felt a little empathy for him and Gram having to take care of Christy and me the past six years since Dad was killed in the car-train crash. Looking at him, in spite of his age and ill health, I thought he was still one of the best spear fishermen around and he had taught me well. I wished I could prove to him I was a good spear fisherman, and maybe tomorrow and the next day we would get along better.

"Gonna take a snooze. Go ahead and put the decoy back into the water and you spear that next fish. Wake me up if you run into any problems, but I know you can handle it." He opened the pot-belly stove and added a couple more logs to the fire. Positioning himself at the end of his bench, he leaned his back against the wall of the shed, pulled a blanket over the top of him and started to fall asleep.

I lowered the decoy back into the icy blue-green water and reached over to the corner of the shed and grabbed my spear. I wrapped the extra rope around my left arm, leaving about six feet coiled up on the icy lake surface next to the fishing hole. I glanced over at Gramps and could tell from his snoring and farting, he was already in dreamland. I leaned over and peered down into the shimmering water hole and saw my reflection on the surface of the water. I forced a smile, but still did not feel very confident. A sudden gust of wind blew against our fishing shed, shaking it and creating a ripple effect on the water in the ice hole. I jumped back at this noise and the water disturbance and began to grow nervous with anticipation. What if I spotted a pike swimming into the hole, threw my spear at it and missed? Gramps would be so pissed. *Please God, help me spear a fish today.*

The minutes ticked by. I looked at my watch and noted it was almost one o'clock. Gramps was continuing to snooze and there was no action going on in the fishing hole. Even the decoy had stopped moving with no lake current pushing against it. The wind had died down, the stove quit its wood crackling sounds and it got quiet.

I reached over to the line holding the decoy and tugged a few times, trying to get some action going. Nothing. I was starting to get a little sleepy myself. I slapped my face and ordered my body to stay awake. I *had* to spear the next fish that poked his nose into the ice cavern. I stared down into the water and noticed the decoy was moving back and forth, almost in a twirling motion as a strong lake current pushed its way past it. I watched the hypnotizing motion, fighting to keep my eyes open. I glanced away from the ice hole and closed my eyes, visualizing a ten-pounder swimming into the ice hole.

When I looked back, I noticed the decoy line dancing back and forth. I stared down into the blue-green water hole and then I saw it. The head of a giant northern pike had inched its way into the perimeter, coming up to within a couple inches of the decoy minnow. The pike's head looked to be at least five inches wide. He was huge...must have been ten or fifteen pounds at least. Gramps would be so proud of me spearing this sucka, and we would have frozen fish for several weeks.

I quietly stood up, arched my spear above my head and cocked back my right arm for the thrust. The giant fish opened his mouth like he was going to gobble up the decoy and at the last second the pike rolled his eyes up and appeared to stare directly up at me. He closed his mouth and looked like he was now actually smiling; a very subtle, but almost demonic smile. I froze in fear and started to lower my spear. *Screw it,* I thought to myself, *do it, Justin, kill the son-of-a-bitch.*

I threw the spear into the water and watched the razor points rip into the flesh of the pike, gushing blood into the water. Yes! Dead-on. The fish lunged away from the ice hole, trailing the spear with him as the rope on the icy floor uncoiled into the water. I looked down in horror, suddenly realizing I had inadvertently stepped inside the coiled rope. It snapped around my ankle, knocked me on my butt onto the icy shed floor and started dragging me, feet first, towards the icy abyss. I screamed for Gramps to help me and glanced over to see him still sound asleep. I grabbed the bench, trying to hold on to something, but this fish was unbelievably strong, continuing to pull me into the fish hole, feet first, and now up to my waist. I turned and grabbed the edge of the ice, digging my fingers into the icy edge. Too late.

The fish pulled me all the way into the water, down the shaft and under the ice covering the lake's surface. I held my breath, fighting off hypothermia from the frigid water as the fish started to tow me towards the deeper and darker area of the lake. I dug my fingernails into the crusty under-surface of the ice, slowing down our forward motion away from the ice hole. A panicked scream exploded from my lungs, encapsulated in air bubbles that bounced off the undersurface ice cover. My only chance for survival would be to claw my way back to the ice hole. I reached down and tried to untie the coiled rope around my ankle. No luck. I was freezing and coughing on the water going into my lungs. I knew then I was going to die under this ice cover, not discovered until spring melted the ice surface of the lake.

Suddenly, our forward motion stopped. I reached down and uncoiled the rope from around my ankle. I turned and saw the light reflecting around our fishing hole, only a few yards away, and started swimming back. I could make it if I could just hold my breath a little while longer. I could do this. I had practiced holding my breath for up to five minutes at our summer swim parties.

As I swam towards the light shaft and my last chance at survival, I glanced back to see the giant five-foot-long fish shake loose the spear and charge towards me, his jaws open, exposing four rows of razor sharp teeth. What the hell? Why was he swimming back to me? I realized then, the decoy was not going to be his lunch. I was! Screaming more bubbles out into the water, I swam like I never have before. Would I make it back to the ice hole in time? I looked back, one last time, to see the monster fish closing in on me, jaws open wide for the kill.

A gust of wind blew against the ice fishing house, shaking the walls and waking me up. I jumped up screaming and realized I was back, not in the water, but inside our warm shed. Gramps bolted up with a surprised look on his face.

"What the hell, Justin, what happened? You spear a fish?"

I stood there, shaking, staring down at the icy blue-green water and at the spear in my hand and the rope coiled on the ice, next to the fishing hole. I thought to myself: *Thank you, God, thank you. It was only a dream.*

"Nah, I thought I saw one, but it swam away before I could throw my spear. Got excited and started yelling, I guess. Sorry."

"It's okay. There'll be another one. Tell you what, I gotta take off a little early. I'll get this fish home to Momma and finish up some work on a car engine for Mr. Peters in town. You stay a little while longer and see if you can spear one more fish for us."

"Sure 'nuff. I'll be fine and promise you I'll spear a pike and be home in a couple hours."

"On my way. I'll take the supplies back with me in the truck. Bring home that second pike and leave your spear and the decoy here. Lock up the door when you leave. Be home before five o'clock. You know it's getting dark out there and the timber wolves are coming out earlier this winter. I heard tell there's not enough food for them and they're gettin' downright vicious, attacking folks and all. Run back home on the lake surface…don't walk on the forest trail. Take you only about fifteen minutes." He stood up, picked up his spear, his blanket and the cooler and went past me to the door. He patted me on the head as he passed by and exited the shed door and closed it again.

"Bye, Gramps. See you in a couple hours or so," I yelled after him. I listened to him start the pickup and drive away. I looked back at the fishing hole with its now darker blue-green water staring back at me and got goose bumps. This was one of the few times I wished Gramps was still next to me.

CHAPTER 5

I stared into the fishing hole, watching the decoy minnow twist and turn with the flowing lake currents. I glanced at my watch, realizing it was four o'clock and past time for me to pack up and leave. Come on, one more fish, so I wouldn't disappoint Gramps and would prove to myself I could really do this. The fire was burning down, the wind outside the shed had reduced to a whisper and I knew darkness was creeping over the horizon.

What was that? Yup, there it was again…the howling. The timber wolves were trekking down the surrounding hills towards the lake.

I stood up to stretch, feigning a spear thrust towards the murky fishing hole. I could barely make out the decoy lure dangling in the water, when it happened. I saw a brown/green yellow-spotted blur dart through the ice perimeter, giving a glancing blow to the decoy minnow, spinning it into a circular pattern. A strike. *He'll be back*. I raised my spear above my head, cocking my arm and the spear points toward the hole and held my breath and waited for the next attack. There it was! The pike lunged at the decoy minnow, taking it into his mouth. With all my pent-up frustration and determination, I heaved the metal spear into the water hole and struck the northern pike dead center, near his top dorsal fin. Thrashing about in the bloodied water, the fish attempted to swim away, but I was prepared for this and reached down to pull back on the attached spear rope. I jerked and tugged on the rope, hand-over-hand, and reeled the rope and spear back up through the fishing hole. I slapped the fish onto the ice floor of the shed, screaming a victory yell.

"Yes! I got you, son-of-a-bitch. I knew I could do this. Thank you, God, or the angels. Whatever, thank you."

I put my foot on top of the twisting, flopping fish and pulled out the spear tongs. I was a little disappointed by the size, probably only a four-pounder or so, but at this juncture of the trip, I would take just about anything. I picked up the pike and dropped it into the bucket container then glanced down at my watch. Past four-thirty and I needed to be hiking back.

I stacked all the supplies into the corner of the shed, put on my heavy jacket, gloves and pulled my stocking cap down over my ears. I checked the stove, determining it was almost out with all the wood burned away. I took one last look around the old fish shed, picked up my fish bucket and before turning off the kerosene lantern, snagged a power beam flashlight. I made my way through the darkened interior, opened the door and stepped out into a very cold and dark world.

I closed the door and snapped shut the padlock and glanced up at black, ominous clouds rolling in from the north. Another snowstorm was zeroing in on us. I turned away from the ice shed and started jogging across the lake towards the house. No sweat. I should be home in less than twenty minutes. But man, it was dark out here, feeling more like nine o'clock at night rather than five.

It was easy to jog on the lake surface following the tire tracks of Gramps ol' pickup truck. Plus the wind had died down and the dark cloud cover kept the temperature above twenty degrees or so. I stopped for a moment, adjusting my glasses secured against my face by my black, woolen stocking cap. I wrapped my scarf around my neck a little tighter and was good to go. I returned to jogging when I heard that chilling sound again. It was a timber wolf howling over at the shoreline of the lake, behind the pine trees, only a few hundred yards away from me.

I stopped to shine my flashlight onto the shoreline and into the pine tree area the howl came from, trying to slow down my nervous breathing. I swept the light back and forth across the tree branches and raspberry bushes. Nothing. No more howling. I started jogging again, faster now, tightly clutching my fish pail and flashlight. Then I heard it…one howling noise followed by a second, back in that same pine tree area near the shoreline. I squinted, anxiously searching for any silhouette of Gram's house ahead of me, at the end of the lake. There it was, probably only fifteen minutes away. I ran faster now, knowing I could make it. Everything was fine.

I quickly glanced back, shocked to see two timber wolves on the lake, lumbering after me. The blood froze in my veins as I exhaled a panicked breath. They were trotting at a steady gait, keeping up with me, about five hundred yards back. This was crazy. They weren't supposed to be out on the open lake. They always hunted their prey inside the forest or along the shoreline. Then I remembered Gramps saying it was a lean year and the wolves were extra hungry this winter. They were trying a new strategy in securing their next meal.

I increased my speed, jogging faster now towards the safety of my home. I looked back to see the two wolves also picking up their speed and actually gaining on me.

Then I heard another howling cry to the left of me, along the shoreline. I quickly turned my flashlight beam in the direction of the sound and illuminated a set of green eyes, glowing back at me. Then the eyes turned into a dark wolf form, running along the shoreline, keeping pace with me. The pack was organizing their attack plan. And I had no gun, no knife or weapons of any kind to defend myself against three wolves. I was quickly running out of options and time to save my life.

Now the shoreline wolf stopped, let out a yip, yip sound and the other two wolves ran over to him. They were standing on the shoreline, behind me, licking each other's faces and staring out at this helpless humanoid, running in vain for his life. It was almost like they were conducting some sort of wolf meeting or strategy on how they were going to take me down. What could I do? Then, I remembered Gramps saying timber wolves did not like fire or strange, unfamiliar noises.

An idea flashed into my desperate, panic-stricken brain. I glanced back to see the wolves still occupied with their kill plan. They were now howling and gazing up towards the other end of the lake. Were they calling in support troops and waiting for them to show up? Now was my chance. I set the fish pail down on the lake and ran like hell to the shoreline. The wolves were still howling for their friends while looking away from my location and did not notice me dashing for the tree cover. I ran in between some dense shrubbery, did a quick visual and spotted a large, broken pine tree branch on the ground. It was about six feet long and probably four feet wide at its bushy girth. It was dried out but still full of heavy pine needles and when I lifted it up, thank God, it was of a light weight. I slung the torn log end over my shoulder and towing the pine branch with me, walked quickly out through the shrubbery and back onto the lake to my fish pail. I glanced over, noticing the wolves were now watching me while cocking their heads to one side, seeming to exhibit...curiosity? As I arrived back at the bucket on the lake, they began trotting over to my location.

Quickly, I stuck my flashlight in my pocket, took hold of my fish bucket and with my free hand, balanced the branch over my shoulder while stepping inside the middle of the bushy pine needles. I began walking. I pulled and drug the pine branch along with me, cloistered inside, following the pickup truck tire tracks. The wolves arrived next to me and immediately started snarling and nipping at my feet and ankles inside the moving pine tree branch. I could tell they were confused by the scraping noise and when they tried to thrust their jaws into the middle of the pine tree cover, some of the needles poked their sensitive noses. They did not give up and redoubled their snapping efforts, determined to snag my foot or ankle. I walked faster, but had to be careful to balance the branch on my shoulder, stay in the middle of the pine needles and hang onto my fish pail. If I fell down or tripped, it would be over for me. I thought about throwing my fish pail out to them for a diversion, but at this point, I was not giving up the fish prize I'd fought so hard to spear. And I thought it was working. Like Gramps said, the wolves were confused by a moving tree and the noise made by the pine branches dragged over the surface of the snow-packed lake surface.

One of the wolves was getting extra brave, pushing his snapping jaws into my enclosure, coming very close to snagging my foot. If he sunk his teeth into my boot, or my ankle, he would lock his jaws down, start to shake my leg, I would fall down and it would be over. I pushed the fish pail down on my arm, reached up and grabbed my wool stocking cap and threw it at one of the snapping wolf jaws. He immediately snatched it off the lake surface, dragging it outside my enclosure and began shaking it back and forth. I listened to another wolf jump over and start fighting him for it. The human scent was driving them crazy. It gave me a momentary reprieve, but they were soon back again, seemingly more angry and determined than before. Maybe they were emboldened by the smell of human flesh and were going in for the final kill. I didn't know how much longer this was going to work.

I looked up to see Gram's house coming clearly into view, with the frozen dock jutting out onto the lake. It was only about five hundred yards away. I was fighting back the tears and started screaming for someone to help me. Would these hunger-crazed wolves follow me clear up to the back porch?

I kept moving forward, my arm aching, ready to break from balancing the pine branch on my shoulder. I was getting weak and dizzy but I knew if I could last for just a few minutes more, I would be on land. The wolves seemed to increase the intensity of their attacks, sensing their dinner was getting away. I was almost home.

I kept screaming, hoping someone would hear me. I thought I could see Gram, peering out the kitchen window. Then, one of the wolves bit into my boot, through to my ankle, dug his paws into the icy surface and started to shake my leg. I felt myself tumble down, spilling out of my pine-branch enclosure, onto the lake.

I put my hands and arms over my face as one of the wolves lunged forward and pounced on me, clamping his jaws down on my thick coat sleeve. He began shaking my arm back and forth while the other two wolves advanced to take their bite out of my legs. I knew I was going to die.

I heard the shot ring out and watched in slow motion as a giant hole ripped through the chest cavity of the wolf on top of me. Blood, fur and gut tissue splattered my face. I pushed the very dead wolf off me, struggled up and heard a second shot and watched one of the other wolves yip in pain. The remaining two were now hightailing it for the opposite shoreline, one limping, obviously hit by a slug in his hind quarter. I turned to see Gramps walking towards me, his 30-30 rifle in hand.

"Justin, you sure believe in living close to the line, don't you. Where were you? Told you to be home over two hours ago."

I ran to him and gave him a big hug…uncomfortable for him, but it felt fantastic to me. Crusty Gramps, always lecturing me.

"Thank you, Gramps, for saving my life. I'm sorry, I should have left the ice shed a long time ago, but wanted to spear at least one fish. Come 'ere, see what I got." I was still trembling, but pulled him over to the fish bucket sitting next to the pine branch on the lake. I reached in, grabbed the fish and proudly displayed my prize.

"Very good, my boy. Your grandma will be happy to cook that one up for dinner tomorrow night. And what's with the pine branch?"

"Remember, Gramps, you talked about using this technique to save yourself from the wolves, many years ago? I just copied your story. You saved my life twice today. Thank you." I hugged him again.

"All right. Next time listen to me and get your butt home when I tell you. None of this would a happened if you did. Get up to the house...supper is waiting on us. You need to clean all that wolf blood off your face so as not to scare Momma. And after you eat, cut up that pine branch and throw it into the cellar storage and we'll use it for kindling," he gruffly instructed.

He turned and I followed him up the embankment to the back porch, dragging the pine branch and carrying my prize northern pike in the bucket. Old Gramps, most of the time, so difficult to figure and so hard to get along with. But today, he was my hero.

CHAPTER 6

"It's not safe for you to stay here much longer. Sheriff Cooper was snooping around last week, asking too many questions. You need to decide what way you are a-going. I think you oughta turn yourself back in and be done with all this. Here, have another piece of fried chicken before your brother eats everything up." Clive handed the plate of chicken across the table to Gusta.

"It's all working out fine, Pa. That south pasture root cellar's doing the job for my second home. Sheriff will never find me there. I'll just hang out, lay low and probably head out next week. Got some friends near Fargo that will put me up for awhile 'til I get my game plan finalized. So, soon as I get word, I'll be moving in with those guys and won't cause you any more trouble."

"Trouble, I remember Trouble. That was your first doggy, you named him Trouble and he had a nice collar and everything," Raymond interjected, reaching across the table for more biscuits. "And the collar had a dog license number,

A1370, I remember that good." Raymond flashed a big, missing-toothed grin at his brother.

"I know I agreed to let you stay on here a spell. But it seems to me, be a better idear to turn yourself in and go finish up your sentence. Lawyer called a few days ago and said if you did, the judge would go easy on you, give you a break on your three-year sentence and you'd be out real soon, a free man again."

"Pa, I'm never going back to that hellhole prison again. There are a couple guys waiting for me to do some bad shit. And the guard I knocked out will have all his guard friends waiting to even the score. You don't know the revenge crap they would take out on me. They could end up killing me. No, Papa, I ain't going back. I'll take my chances out here; survive in the woods if I have to. And my friends in Fargo will help me out." Gusta stood, clenching his fists together, tightening his muscular arms and began pacing the adjoining family room floor.

"All right, son, but I'm a warning ya, if Cooper finds you hiding out here, he will put a world of hurt on your pa, and I may end up in prison with you. Come on, Raymond, finish stuffing your face. We gotta get a move on and check those beaver traps down by the lake." Raymond gulped down his last morsel of food and pushed away from the table, brushing his long greasy dark hair away from his unshaven, unwashed face.

"What the hell!" Gusta glanced out the front window, watching Sheriff Cooper's patrol car turn off the highway onto the dirt road and drive towards their house.

"The sheriff is here, Pa. I'm hightailing it out back to the root cellar." Gusta grabbed his jacket, hit the back door and slammed through it on a dead run through the dried-out cornfield towards the woods. He didn't bother to look back, but picked up his pace once he broke through the clearing and angled towards the first small rise, off to his left, at the forest entrance. The root cellar would be in front of him, buried in the hillside, completely hidden by a dense growth of raspberry bushes. He pushed aside a section of the berry shrubbery, pulled open the trap doors and clamored down the steps, into the darkened cellar, pulling the shrubbery-covered doors closed behind him.

"Howdy, Sheriff, didn't expect to see you so soon in this neck of the woods. Come on in." Clive ushered Sheriff Cooper into his front room. "Raymond, make yourself useful and start clearing off the dinner table." Clive motioned for the sheriff to sit down in the family room, nervously glancing at Raymond clearing off the table, which included three place settings.

Sheriff Cooper took off his hat, ran his large hands through his dark, crew-cut hair and set his large, slightly overweight frame down on the available sofa. He turned his intense dark eyes towards Clive and forced a half-smile across his stern, military-bearing face. He glanced over at Raymond clearing off the table. "How's the hunting season going, Clive? You boys baggin' your limits?"

"You know us, Sheriff; we always manage to get our limits...and then some."

"Yeah, I know that and no problem. Don't go bragging 'bout it to your neighbors. Anyway, dropping by, Clive, 'cause I heard rumors from one of your neighbors, thought they saw your son, Gusta, on your property last week. Any truth to that?"

"Be straight with you, Sheriff. My boy did stop by last week on his way to stay with some friends. I kept telling him to turn himself in and finish out his sentence to get back to help his pa and brother run our place here. But Sheriff Cooper, he's a feared of going back and getting beat up or even killed. So he moved on to his friends' place. Only stayed here a day. I talked with his attorney about all this and he told me the judge would be lenient and all if Gusta turned himself in. So I'm trying, Sheriff, doing what I can, but my boy don't listen to his pa anymore."

Sheriff Cooper nodded at hearing the story, focused for any tell-tale body language giveaways. "Hope you're being honest with me, Clive. I would hate to arrest you for harboring a fugitive. All this could get you into a heap of trouble."

"Gusta used to have a doggy named Trouble, lived right here with a nice collar that had the number A1370," Raymond interjected as he wiped down the kitchen table.

"Okay, hush, Raymond. The sheriff don't want to hear about no dog."

Sheriff Cooper stood up, walked over to Raymond, placed his hands on his shoulders and moved in to stand face-to-face with him. "And how 'bout you, Raymond? Have you seen Gusta lately?"

Clive caught his breath and broke into a sweat, staring at his older, mentally challenged son. He knew it was difficult for Raymond to lie.

Raymond hung his head, averting the intensity of the sheriff's visual interrogation. "Gusta is gone. He is gone," he quietly replied. The sheriff seemed satisfied and removed his hands from Raymond's shoulders.

"Okay, gents, will leave you be. Remember, Clive, the lawyer got the judge to agree to this reduced sentence compromise, but only if Gusta gives himself up…soon. Can't take all year deciding this. Let your son know that. And by the way, while I'm here, all right if I check around your property a bit? I can go back to town and get a search warrant, but it'd be easier now since I'm here. Not that I don't believe you and all."

"Be my guest, Sheriff. Like I said, we got nothin' to hide." He shook Sheriff Cooper's hand while leading him to the front door. The sheriff exited the door, walked down the porch steps and slid into the front seat of his cruiser. They waved good-bye as the police car angled off the driveway and onto a dirt road leading to the back of Clive's property, directly towards the south field root cellar.

Gusta finished securing the overhead folding doors tightly shut above the steps leading down to the root cellar entrance. He knew the raspberry bushes outside concealed the wooden, folding doors completely and even if the person knew the exact location, it was difficult to find the opening. He continued to walk down the concrete steps toward the metal entry door, shining his flashlight in front of him. He pushed open the entry door into a darkened, damp-smelling cave-like dwelling and closed and locked the door behind him.

He spotted the kerosene lantern with his flashlight, found some matches and lit the lantern that sat on a small table next to a makeshift, mattress-only bed. He glanced around his eight-by-ten-foot enclosure with its dirt floor, dirt walls, plywood ceiling and shelves lined with bottles of berries, vegetables, jerky and marinating venison .He reached up and took hold of a canteen and drank a long swig of cool, refreshing water, thinking how depressing all this was...almost like being back in prison. But tonight, he would take his rifle and knife out and do a little nocturnal hunting. The wolves and bears did not worry him. He needed to kill something in preparation of tracking

53

down a special prey next week. He was looking forward to leaving his pa's place and settling one last score with his cousin, Justin.

CHAPTER 7

"Minneapolis, St. Paul. End of the line. Please be careful exiting the bus and be sure to take all your personal belongings with you. Thank you for choosing Greyhound Bus Lines."

I stood up, stretched, and pulled down my suitcase from the overhead compartment. I then peered out the window, searching for Eric in the crowd of people waiting at the bus terminal lobby entrance. Yes, there he was, glancing up at the bus while talking with his grandfather. I pushed my way through the narrow aisle of the bus, bounded down the steps and sauntered over to my best friend in this whole world.

"Well, little brother, you finally got here. Bus was running late and Gramps was getting concerned." Eric held out his hand to shake mine and then pulled me into a bear hug. Man, this guy was strong.

"Yeah, the roads were a little slippery with the new snow, so the driver took his time. But it's great seeing you again, fellow knight. You've grown two inches since last summer. And hello, Mr. Hodson. You and your wife doing all right?"

"My wife and I are doing wonderful, Justin. So good seeing you again. We have missed our cabin up on Pickerel Lake and all the great barbeque parties at your grandparents' home. Looking forward to next summer."

"So am I. And Eric, your sweetheart Robyn said she misses you so much and wanted me to give you a big, slobbery kiss for her. Pucker up, big brother." I grabbed Eric's head with both hands and pulled his face towards mine, pursing my lips. I could not keep a straight face and broke out laughing. He reached up and pulled my stocking cap down over my face and started laughing while saying something about it not being funny.

"Come on, boys, time's a wasting and momma has a delicious lunch prepared for us back at the house. We should be there by noon."

He turned and walked towards their Lincoln Town car in the front section of the bus depot parking lot. We followed, punching at each other, discussing Robyn and my girl Audrey and the fun times we all had together last summer. We climbed into the backseat of the luxurious Lincoln and Mr. Hodson eased it out onto the highway towards their home in Albert Lea.

"Well, tell me all the news. How do you like Park Rapids Junior High? You see the cousins every day at school? You still have to move to the Cities this next January with your mom and her new boyfriend?" Eric asked.

"Lots of news. Like I told you on the phone last week, I got this note from Audrey. They are living in Duluth now and she still cannot give out the exact address. Her dad won't allow it with all his secretive government work concerning our giant fish out there in Pickerel Lake and our pictures and everything.

She didn't really explain and it's all still kind of mysterious with their family leaving their house suddenly, at the end of last summer. But she mentioned to Robyn about the possibility of the four of us getting together in Park Rapids, maybe on a week-end, sometime before Christmas."

"Man, that would be fantastic. Let me know, my grandparents could drive us up to my Aunt Isabelle's place in PR and we could have a day out, with our ladies."

"You're on. I'll tell Robyn and she'll work out the details. So, fill me in on how we're going to check out the Nickelson Brothers."

"I've done some poking around about these creeps, their strip club in the Cities, and put together a game plan for our detective work this evening."

I listened intently to my best friend's latest information on Randy's possible killers, the Nickelson Brothers. I glanced out the car window, watching the snow-covered pine trees rush by while listening to Eric outline our breaking and entering strategy. It all made sense, yet sounded a little crazy and dangerous. But that was my best friend's MO, always living on the edge. Only fifteen years old, but with his six-foot physique, karate skills and supreme self-confidence, he was always ready to take on the world.

"We're here, boys. Go on inside and wash up. Momma is waiting on us and you can finalize your plans after lunch."

The car pulled into the driveway, I grabbed my suitcase, and Eric and I jumped out of the back of the car and walked up to their front porch, pushing through the front door. Man, I hadn't been in their house in a couple years and was struck again by what a spacious, beautiful home it was. And just for a few seconds, I was envious of how rich Eric and his grandparents were. Then, Mrs. Hodson came up to greet us and gave me a welcoming hug.

"Justin, such a pleasure to welcome you into our home again. I hope your bus trip to the Cities was pleasant. Leave your jackets and suitcase in the front room. You must be starving. Come into the dining room...lunch is served." Such a sweet lady, but I was reminded, in spite of her small stature and friendly twinkling eyes, that she was in charge of this family.

We sat down to a great meal of fried Northern Pike, mashed potatoes, gravy, sweet corn-on-the-cob and fresh biscuits. Mrs. Hodson could cook as good as my own grams. She asked me about school, my sister Christy and the latest on the Pickerel Lake mystery fish. I was careful to say just enough, especially about our mystery fish, looking over at Eric for visual guidance.

The lunch was great and then Eric's grandma brought out some hot, steaming home-made apple pie with ice cream a la mode. I was stuffed but forced myself to eat the dessert. All the food I ate and I remained a weak, skinny guy with a struggling, still developing, self-image...totally opposite from my adopted big brother. I glanced over at Eric, thankful again for a friend who more than made up for my personal deficiencies and was still training me for a more positive, better life ahead.

"Thanks, Grams, that was super delicious," Eric announced. "Now Justin and I need to go to my room and finish up some planning." He pushed away from the table and motioned for me to follow him.

"Thank you, Mrs. Hodson, for that great lunch," I added.

"You are certainly welcome, Justin. It is so nice to have you visit for the weekend. You are always welcome in our home."

I excused myself from the table and followed Eric to his bedroom, snagging my suitcase along the way. He closed the door behind us; I tossed my suitcase on his bed and he pulled over a couple chairs to his study desk.

"You are not going to believe what else I discovered about Randy's killers, the Nickelson brothers, and their strip club back in the Cities. Listen to this."

My buddy went on to explain how on one trip to the Cities, he and his grandpa waited in their Lincoln, across the street from the night club, hidden from view, observing the activity. There was a light snow falling and Eric said he watched one of the brothers go into their storage building at the back of the club, remove a large overcoat and snow boots and then enter through a back security door into the club. Eric explained tonight would be our chance to sneak into that club storage shed, find the boots with the cutout wedge in one of the heels, look for a red and green flannel hunting shirt and take a bunch of pictures. We could then turn over the photos to Sheriff Cooper, contributing additional evidence linking the brothers to Randy's murder. I listened, thinking it might work, if we were lucky.

"And Justin, while you're thinking all that over, take a look at this." He went over to his dresser, pulled out a fantasy and science fiction magazine and tossed it on my lap. "Check out the cover and the caption and page thirty-seven."

I looked down and read aloud the front cover headline: "Giant Fish Caught on Film. Real or Fake?" I turned to page thirty-seven and there, in full color, was a picture of our monster Pickerel Lake fish lunging out of the water, snagging our bird bait, with an accompanying story. What a beautiful shot of our fish.

"See, they didn't get it published in Time or Look magazine like they wanted, but got it into a sci-fi magazine. That's our picture…one of the three we sold to the brothers for that five hundred dollars. A picture like the one that got Randy murdered."

"Wow, that is something," I whispered out loud. "But it's still difficult to believe Randy was killed over a stupid fish photo."

"Well, it happened, and it's time to bring all the killers to justice. That asshole Gusta got a jail sentence for his part, thanks to your strategy with the traps. Now it is the Nickelson Brothers' turn for payback."

"Sounds great to me. You have a camera and your lock-picking device?"

"As my gramps would say, darn tootin' I do. And Gramps is ready to drive us back up to the Cities before it gets too dark and before their strip club opens at eight p.m. You ready, my detective partner?"

"Let's do it!" I replied. I was excited, but a little concerned. I remembered Audrey, last summer, when we said good-bye and she warned me about being careful in our detective work around the Nickelson Brothers. I wondered to myself, if they caught us, what would they do?

"Right on!" Eric said. "We are going to nail those sons-a-bitch's asses to the wall. Give me a high five. We'll leave in an hour."

CHAPTER 8

Mr. Hodson pulled up across the street from the Nickelson brothers' strip lounge on North Hennepin Avenue, his Lincoln partially hidden behind some curbside elm trees. It was already past five o'clock and the brothers would probably be arriving in an hour or so to open the club. The clock was ticking. Eric and I eased out of the car and quietly closed the door.

"Be careful, boys. I'll stay out of sight here across the street, keeping an eye out for you. But at any problem at all, you give me a high sign. I got my permit to carry ol' Betsy here, just in case," he said, holding up his thirty-eight caliber pistol to emphasize the point.

"We'll be okay. I have your metal flashlight with us and you know I can take care of any physical confrontation. We're just gonna take a couple pictures and be right back." Eric gave him that big self-confident grin, patted his gramps on the shoulder and we waved good-bye while crossing the street.

"Eric, I don't see any storage shed by their club," I said.

I glanced at the large neon sign flashing the Kitty Lounge, noticed some dark clouds rolling in from the west and caught sight of a couple vagrants noisily rummaging through the trash bin in front of an alley. The sounds of bottles and cans being tossed against the side of the trash can echoed across the street. I was getting a little nervous. I had heard stories about Hennepin Avenue here in the Cities and it had the reputation of being a dangerous place to walk through, especially at night. And here we were, two young teenagers, going to break into a storage shed and take pictures of some snow boots that hopefully were there, and then turn the photos over to the sheriff for possible evidence connected to Randy's murder? Did we really did have the balls for this crazy detective caper?

"Don't start worrying now. We have to go in the back of the club, near the alley. That's where the storage shed is located. And don't pay any attention to the bums on the street. They're drunk and won't mess with us, knowing the police patrol this area regularly."

We continued walking around to the back of the club, turned the corner by the alley and there it was...just like Eric said it would be. The storage shed was connected to the back of the club building, with a nice big entry door and a large, keyed padlock securing the door handle. This was going to be our first challenge.

"No problem," Eric said. "I got my trusty, rusty lock-picking device and I can open that padlock quicker than, as my gramps would say, two shakes of a lamb's tail. All you have to do is hold the flashlight steady for me and keep an eye out for any curiosity seekers that may come our way."

We quickly approached the shed door and Eric pulled out his special lock-picking device while I shined the flashlight down on his job. I glanced around to make sure no one was watching or approaching us. For some reason, I happened to notice a large clump of choke cherry bushes at the back corner of the storage shed and made a mental note of their location.

Eric was twisting and clicking the picks inside the padlock as the minutes ticked by. No luck. It was not opening. Finally, he let out a gasp of frustration and removed the lock picks. He flashed me a scowl.

"Doing something wrong. I've done this before, on this type of lock, and it should work. Let me think about this a minute."

While listening to Eric's review of the situation, I glanced up the alley and noticed a vagrant peering around the corner of the trash bin, watching our activity. Sporting a full beard, disheveled hair and soiled, tattered clothes, he began stumbling towards us with a weird smile on his face. I nudged Eric, directing his attention towards the approaching bum.

"Oh boy," Eric responded as the large, unsteady man staggered towards us. He motioned for me to remain calm while he started moving towards our curious visitor. I expected Eric to knock the guy out with one of his karate chops to the back of the intruder's neck. Instead, he reached into his pocket and pulled out a half-pint of cheap whiskey and held it by his side.

"What you boys doing? Trying to steal a key so as to come back later and see the naked girls?" The bum started laughing.

"Nah, my uncle, Mr. Nickelson, owns this place and me and my friend here are going sledding tomorrow and need some thermal gloves from this storage shed. Said we could use them and we're on a tight schedule and didn't want to bother him. Anyway, my good man, don't tell anyone we're here and I'll have a little reward for you." Eric held out the half-pint bottle to the bum. The man licked his lips a couple times, came forward and reached out and grabbed for the bottle. Eric pulled it back, just out of his reach.

"Go on down the alley to that park bench over there and enjoy your drink in peace and quiet. Don't hang around here or you may have to share your good fortune with one of your friends. Know what I mean?" Eric instructed the staggering man.

"That makes a heap of sense...I'll be on my way. Good luck in finding your gloves." Eric handed the bum the whiskey and he unscrewed the cap, raised the bottle in a toasting gesture, took a long swig, smiled again and shuffled past us towards the distant park bench.

"Wow, Eric. That was cool. Thought at first you would take him out with one of your karate moves. Where'd you come up with the whiskey?"

"Actually, my gramps' idea. And remember, you never use martial arts except as a last resort to defend yourself. Otherwise, use your brain to figure out the solution to the problem. And like my gramps said, distracting these bums with liquor is like throwing red, raw meat to watch dogs guarding a property. It worked, right? Come on, back to the padlock. I have another idea on opening this suckka."

We moved back to the padlocked door, glancing over our shoulder to make sure there were no more visitors. It was getting dark now. I checked my watch to see it was almost six o'clock. We were running out of time.

"I was only using two picks before, but got to thinking...I think this one takes three picks to open. Need your help. You focus the flashlight beam on the lock, and with your other hand hold an L pin steady inside the lock while I work the other two picks."

He stuck the L pin inside the keyhole of the lock, rotating it until it snapped into place, and instructed me to keep it there. I held it firmly between my fingers and with the other hand, focused the flashlight. He pushed the other two lock pins inside the keyhole and began a twisting motion. Almost immediately, the padlock snapped open.

"Bravo, my assistant break-in artist. Entrance is granted," Eric laughed.

He pulled off the lock, placed it in his jacket pocket and led the way into the darkened shed. I swept the flashlight beam in front of us and scouted the walls while Eric closed the door behind us and pulled a ceiling cord, turning on a dim, overhead light. We adjusted our eyes to our surroundings and followed the flashlight beam as it illuminated file boxes stacked everywhere. Over in a corner was an open closet with heavy gear, a red and green flannel jacket, ski pants and bingo: a collection of snow boots stacked on the floor of the closet.

"Here they are. Turn the boots over while I get the camera ready." We upended all the boots and finally came to the last pair, a size thirteen, and there it was, the gouged-out section in the heel. It matched the boot print I saw in the bloodied snow next to Randy's body.

"Okay, wait a minute. Have to prove our location." He pulled down a file box with a label on the outside stating 'Nickelson Brothers Kitty Club' and this year's date. He set the box down next to the turned-up boots, leaning them together, adjusted his camera and flashed several photos of the boot evidence and the interior of the shed, including the flannel jacket in the background. We put the file box and boot exactly back into place and Eric patted the camera…now safely returned to his jacket pocket. "We have some key evidence to turn over to Sheriff Cooper so he can get a search warrant, come down here and check out the jacket for blood stains, pick up the boots and, with Gusta's confession, he can nail these assholes to the wall. Come on, we're outta here."

We turned off the overhead light and pushed our way through the shed entry door, double-checking the area around the building to make sure no one was watching. We closed the door, put the padlock back on and turned to walk down the alley to the street, when suddenly the connecting door to the club began to open and a woman's laughter erupted into the cold, night air. Too late. We couldn't make it back down the alley or we would be spotted for sure. I grabbed Eric's coat sleeve and pulled him with me towards that clump of brush by the edge of the storage shed that I had noted before. We ran to the side of the shed and ducked down behind the protective shrubbery just as the back club entrance door swung open and one of the brothers, Steve Nickelson, stepped outside with a show girl hanging on his arm. We were well hidden, but could still observe the action in front of us.

"It's a beautiful night, Candy, and over an hour before the show starts. How 'bout we go into the shed and fuck for ten minutes, get you hot and lubricated, so you can turn on those customers and rake in all that tip money." They both took long drags on their cigarettes and started laughing.

"Honey, sweety, I'd love to, but it'll mess up my nice outfit I took so long to pick out. Have to change and everything. Maybe later?" she responded by pushing her lips up to his and, reaching down, grabbed his crouch. He then placed his hand on top of her sequined show bra and pulling it down, allowed two very large breasts to flop out, totally exposed. She struggled to pull her show bra back up while the brother fondled one of

66

her breasts. They continued laughing even when Candy slapped his hand and finished pulling up her bra, stuffing her tits back into the bra cups.

I looked over at Eric and gulped while he smiled back at me and showed a two thumbs-up sign back to me. I punched him on the shoulder.

"Okay, doll baby. Tonight after the show, I'll send the other girls on home and have a little rendezvous with you in your dressing room for a cock and bull story. You know, lots of cock and no bull." They started laughing again, flicked away their cigarettes and pushed their way back into the club house, slamming the door behind them.

Eric and I squatted there, for a moment, behind the shrubbery, breathing hard...I guess from a combination of the danger and excitement of our detective mission and the free side show we'd witnessed. We stood back up and visually checked our immediate surroundings one more time before leaving our hiding place.

"Enough fantasy time. We got the evidence. Let's get the hell out of here and head back to my gramps car."

We quickly walked out of the alley and up to the corner of Hennepin Street. We could see Eric's gramps sitting in the Lincoln. He waved at us. We crossed the street, passing another Kitty lounge girl on her way to the club's front door. She turned towards us and whispered a very sexy hello. Eric and I both glanced up to respond and just before she moved away, I saw something that sent a quivering chill up my spine. Naw, had to be my imagination; that was not what I thought it was. I almost choked on the spit in my throat, and I grabbed Eric's arm.

"Eric, look! Did you see that? God, did you see that?" I exclaimed, shaking.

"Little brother, that had to be our imagination working overtime. That's all."

"What imagination? Did you see it too?"

He hesitated a few seconds before responding.

"Don't say anything. Don't tell me what you saw. Just our imagination." But I knew I saw that strip girl's face change into something weird.

We slid into the back seat of the Lincoln, said hello to his gramps and told him everything went smoothly.

"Who are these Nickelson brothers, really, and what kind of dance club girls change their faces like that?" Eric blurted out. "Maybe there is a deeper, hidden reason they were so interested in the monster fish from Pickerel Lake and were willing to kill Randy for those photos."

"And maybe if we turn this boot photo evidence over to Sheriff Cooper and he harasses them with a search warrant, the brothers will put two and two together and come after us to stop us from doing any more investigative work," I added.

Mr. Hodson started up the car and pulled onto the highway leading back to their home.

Proceed with caution, I thought to myself. Audrey's warning came back into my mind again about being very careful doing our investigative work around the Nickelson brothers. And now after seeing that club girl's strange face, I felt there could be more complex reasons for Randy's murder and why the Nickelson Brothers were so interested in the photos of the giant fish in Pickerel Lake. Somehow, it was all tied in together and we were only beginning to scratch the surface.

CHAPTER 9

Audrey finished her letter to Justin, folded it into the envelope addressed to Robyn and stared out her bedroom window across the snow-covered yard to the house next door. They were strange neighbors, always asking questions since her family moved here at the end of last summer. Her dad said to be careful, that it was still not safe to say too much about their situation. How she hated that word…situation. Tears welled up in her eyes when she thought back to last summer at the lake with Justin, Eric, Robyn and poor Randy before he was killed. Now she was in a new, strange location, in a house that was inferior to their previous home in Park Rapids and in a new school that she hated. All because of her dad and his secret job with the government and that giant fish in Pickerel Lake. This was her current "situation."

"Audrey dear, dinner is ready. Come down and help me set the table. Your father will be home any moment," her mother called up to her.

Audrey stood up, tucked the letter into her pocket and went into the bathroom to put on her smiley face. She stared at her image for a moment, ran a brush through her ash blond tresses, put on some fresh lipstick and leaned in to kiss the mirror. She raised her lipstick tube up to the mirror, drew an arrow to her lip image and wrote next to the arrow, "For Justin."

"Okay, mom, be right down." She skipped down the stairs and into the dining room, gave her mom a quick kiss on the cheek and began setting the plates and silverware on the table. Then she set out a steaming pot roast, some veggies, a green salad and three glasses of ice water. She listened to her mom humming a Broadway tune while they finished up the table setting. She regarded her mom with renewed admiration for remaining positive and taking care of the family in spite of their mystery-shrouded relocation debacle.

"Mom, do you still miss our home back in Park Rapids or you prefer Duluth now?"

Her mom stopped for a moment, took Audrey's hands and, misty-eyed, looked into her daughter's face. Donna's soft brown hair was complemented her youthful face, hazel eyes and confident, peaceful aura. She struggled to smile, not able to hide the frown lines burrowing deeper into her forehead.

"We will probably never quite recover from moving out of our house in the middle of the night and later selling our home and our furniture. But both of us made a commitment to stand by your father and support him in his difficult, unusual job with the government. I know you miss your wonderful friends at the lake, but Audrey, have a little faith. Things will improve soon. I know they will." She squeezed Audrey's hands, flashed that confident mom smile and turned back to the kitchen.

Audrey felt better and had a strange sensation that yes, their situation would improve soon.

"The dessert is almost ready, your dad's favorite…fresh peach cobbler. I think I hear him at the door now."

Audrey smiled and headed over to the front door that was opened by Robert. "Hello, my lovely Audrey. How was your day?"

Her father came into the room, gave his daughter a quick hug, hung up his beige trench coat and removed the snow boot slip-ons from his shoes.

Audrey assured him it was a wonderful day before they went into the dining room where he greeted his wife, Donna, and they all sat down at the dining room table.

"Looks delicious as usual and I am starved," Robert said. "And I have a major announcement for our family, in particular for you, Audrey, which will bring some joy back into this household." He hesitated and it got quiet while everyone filled their plates.

"Well, what is it, Dad? I wrote a sad letter to Robyn and Justin and I need some good news about now."

"I can only tell you a portion of the good news. You know our agency classifies most information as secret. My department wants me, us, to take a week-end and go back to Park Rapids and while staying low key, under the radar, perform additional research on the mystery fish at Pickerel Lake. I may need to talk with Justin and Eric again, and Audrey, you can spend some time with your friends." He winked as he glanced over at his daughter.

"Dad, are you kidding? I love you, I love you" Audrey shrieked, jumping up from the table and grabbing her dad, hugging him around the neck.

"Okay, daughter, I can tell you are happy about this announcement." He untangled her arms from around his neck and she sat back down at the table.

"But Robert, I thought we had to stay hidden in this quasi-witness protection program because it's so dangerous for us," Donna said. "We were required to sell our house and furniture. What was the reason for that?"

"Yes Dad, why the big move and now we can go back for a week-end? And will it be safe? AndWhere will we stay?"

"Let me explain as best as I can at this point." Robert continued eating while his wife and Audrey waited for a response.

"When we left our home in Park Rapids last summer, it was a necessary move, because at that time we were in grave danger. I can tell you this now, due to our knowledge of the giant fish photos, combined with my government position, the agency received a warning that anti-American forces would try and kidnap us and use any means to gain more information. I was later told we barely escaped with our lives and at that time, our secret move was necessary."

"Dad...over some photos of a fish?" Audrey asked.

"Audrey, our agency believes this monster fish has been genetically produced or altered by a DNA code procedure, either by nature or by man, and our government and other governments want to capture that fish and learn the secret of that alteration. You and your friends may think this is a game, but believe me. It is very serious business and has massive security implications for our country."

"So, are Justin and Eric in danger also?" Audrey asked.

"No, not now," Robert replied. "In the last few months, an article about this fish has appeared in a sci-fi magazine complete with pictures and an accompanying story. The spotlight of the press is all over this and it appears two brothers, night club owners in the Cities, are also involved in this ongoing saga. So, our agency and our foreign counterparts are maintaining a low profile and the kidnapping threats have dissipated. Until next spring, at least."

"What's happening next spring, Robert?" Donna asked.

"Sorry. That's another one of those can't-discuss-right-now issues. But in the meantime, the agency said it would be safe to take a week-end, go back to Park Rapids and stay with your sister. And if we are quiet, under the radar, Audrey can spend some time with her friends, while I continue my research."

"Wow! Sounds wonderful to me. When can we go, Dad?"

"Next week-end would be good. Christmas is just around the corner and we have to do this before the holidays."

"So Robert, it's safe to visit my sister Helen? It won't put her in any danger?"

"Totally safe, sweetheart. You can visit Helen while I perform my follow-up research in the Park Rapids area. Audrey, we will invite your friends over for a Sunday luncheon. I just want to ask them a couple questions about the fish. Our agency knows they sold some pictures to those brothers in the Cities. And by the way, daughter, did you go up the lake in a boat and assist Justin and Eric in their fish-photo-caper?" Robert stopped eating and stared at his daughter.

"Yes I did, Dad. AndIt was not dangerous, but exciting and mysterious, kind of like your job. And the best photo, I snapped with Eric's camera."

"Sounds okay, harmless enough, I guess," replied Donna. "I miss our home in Park Rapids."

"One more piece of information, sweetheart. The agency ended up not selling our home. They only leased it out for a year. If this giant fish problem is resolved next spring, as planned, we might be able to get our home back."

Tears came into Donna's eyes as she reached out to take hold of her husband's hand. "That would be wonderful, Robert."

"And I could go back to school at Park Rapids. Yes! Yes!" Audrey jumped up from the table, hugged her dad again and danced around the room.

Audrey pulled out the letter to Robyn at the writing desk. She took out a pen and added a note to the bottom of the letter to Justin: "Will see you next week-end. I'll call with follow-up details. Love, Audrey." She came back into the dining room contemplating this new situation, her favorite word now, this new situation that sounded so wonderful.

CHAPTER 10

The aroma of the turkey that was roasting in the oven wafted throughout the entire house, increasing my appetite at least ten times over. I kicked off my snow boots at the front door, hung up my jacket and was almost knocked over by a flurry of blond ringlets dancing into my arms.

"Justin, bad boy, where have you been? I looked everywhere for you. Today you promised we could go sledding on the ski-jump hill." Christy locked her fingers behind my neck in her famous little sister bear hug and, smiling with her confident, radiating cherub face, waited for my confirmation. With her laughing and not-letting-go-lock on my neck, I waddled to the nearest couch and slung my albatross-like little sister onto the soft pillows and started the tickling defense. She finally let me go.

"Okay, prissy missy, because it is Thanksgiving and I'm in a good mood, we'll go sledding for your first time, on the very dangerous, ski-jump hill. How does that sound?"

"Perfect. And this year, you promised I could do the ski-jump bump all by myself." She returned to the neck-lock procedure for another minute and I defended with the tickling response and then we both sat on the edge of the couch, catching our breath.

"Don't take too long, my dears. Remember, your mom and Kyle will be here in about an hour for our Thanksgiving dinner." Sweet Grams patted down her flour-coated apron and smiled over at us while finishing the dining room table setting.

"Gram, we're only gonna slid for a little while. It's warm out, the snow is getting slippery and it's a perfect time for sledding. 'Sides, Mom's always late and we're gonna see them all day," Christy replied.

I put my hand on her knee and gave her that tone-it-down scowl followed by a big smile and a final tickle. She started laughing again and we stood up and went through the kitchen towards the connecting storage shed.

"All right, we're only going out for a quick downhill racing adventure and will be back by the time Mom arrives. Gram, anything else you need help with?" I asked.

"No, everything is ready. Christy helped me set the table. When you're done sledding, tell your grandpa to come in from the garage and clean up," she added.

"Okay, will do. Come on, Christy, let's put our cold weather gear on and head for the ski slopes." We opened the kitchen door to the storage shed, donned our respective jackets, boots, gloves and stocking caps and stepped past the outer shed door into a brilliant, white, winter wonderland. I couldn't believe it. We had gotten another six inches of snow last night, on top of a two-foot base. But like Christy said, it was warming up and the top of the new white stuff was melting, producing a perfect, slippery sliding surface.

We trudged over to the outdoor storage shed, where I unlocked the padlocked door and pulled out my beautiful, forty-two inch Red Ryder sled. We had other round plastic sleds, a couple toboggans and even a set of old skis, but my Red was best for racing down ol" ski-jump hill.

"You sure you're ready for this, my little, big eight-year-old sister? This ol" sled picks up a lot of speed going down that hill, and you do realize, when you hit the ski-jump bump at the bottom, you could be zooming through the air at over fifty miles per hour, airborne, before landing on the lake surface."

"I'm big now and I can handle it, Mr. Justin. 'Sides, you are a worry wart and you have more warts than an old toad." She laughed at her made-up joke.

We marched away from the house towards the frozen lake and the first hill at an inlet point covered with a cluster of majestic pine trees. I could now spot the ski-jump bump and remembered back a few weeks ago when all the visiting cousins helped me build it. We packed it together with melting snow and surface ice slush from the lake and after a couple hours, had a snow mound over six feet high and eight feet wide with rounded corners. It was positioned exactly between the bottom of the hill and the edge of the lake. We tried the old skis on it first, but they picked up too much speed and nobody was expert enough on skis to jump the ski bump. The plastic sleds did all right, but only with my Red Ryder could you stay on course, hit the bump and become airborne before gliding onto the snow-covered lake surface.

I glanced down at Christy, watching her intent stare at the large mound of packed snow as we began our ascent to the top of the one hundred foot hill. We continued climbing while I tugged on the sled rope, pulling my Red up over the crest of the hill. We stood still for a moment, catching our breath while taking in the winter vista below us. I looked out over the quiet, majestic Pickerel Lake and spied Eric's cabin in the distance, on the other side of the lake. Man, I missed my best friend. Especially since returning home from our exciting and dangerous detective caper at the brothers' Kitty lounge in the Cities. And now, the detective gang was all going to get together this week-end and I would see Audrey again. It seemed almost too good to be true. But, back to the present. I focused on my little sister doing this sled thing right and making sure she stayed safe during the jump.

"Okay, prissy missy. Watch me first and pay attention to the instructions. You lie flat, belly down on the sled, and keep your face behind the nose of the sled and set your hands firmly and comfortably on the steering handles. Keep your legs inside, on top of the sled with your boots pointing down at the back of the sled, ready to drag them into the surface of the snow in case you get going too fast. This is a small hill but you should have just enough speed when you hit the jump bump at the bottom that you will become airborne then land on the surface of the lake and coast. Now, pay attention, stay here and watch me closely."

She nodded her head and stepped to the side. I lay down on top of the sled, aligning my body in the stated position. I grabbed the steering handles, glanced down the hill and with nervous anticipation, kicked off. I started slow at first and then picked up speed as the new-fallen surface snow flew onto my face, covering my glasses. For a second, I was blinded and prayed the sled would follow the previous trail dug towards the ski jump. The wind blew away the snow from my face and I saw the jump bump race towards me as I reached the bottom of the hill.

The loose snow was exploding around the sled when I hit the perimeter of the bump, glided across the top and flew, arching out over the surface of the frozen lake. I glide-landed on the one foot and a cushion of snow, stuck out my leg from the sled, dragged my boot in the snow and spun the sled around 180 degrees to stop, facing the hill again. I stood, watching Christy jump up and down, listening to her unique laugh-scream outburst, as she waved at me. Yes sir, perfect downhill approach, like a bird in flight, with a flawless landing. I pumped my fist in the air and shouted a half-dozen yeses walking back towards the hill. Now it would be Christy's turn.

I tugged the sled back up the hill, lined it up facing downhill and positioned Christy on top of it. I told her to wait while I ran back down to stand next to the ski-jump bump. I wanted to give her last minute directions in case she was not on target with the approach. But I was kidding myself. Once she started down that hill, there was not much I could do to correct anything. I guess I wanted to be downhill in case she messed up, crashed the sled and I could be there to comfort her.

"Okay, prissy missy," I yelled back up the hill. "Push yourself to the edge, start down the hill, dragging your boot toes in the snow. Half-way down, let her rip and go full-speed. Aim for the middle of the ski-jump." I said a little prayer and crossed my fingers. This would be a great experience for her, but it could be dangerous, too. Yet I knew she was tougher than she appeared.

"Geronimo!" she yelled as the Red Ryder tipped over the edge of the precipice and started down the slope. The snow was spraying up behind her from her boot dragging, slowing down the speed of the sled. Then, half-way down the hill, she lifted her boots up and the sled rocketed towards the ski-jump bump. She was going faster than I did because I had packed down the snow trail for her. My heart started racing. Please Lord, not too fast. Her sled reached the ski-jump bump, raced across the top of it and launched into a graceful, slow-motion airborne arch, plopping down onto the thick, snow-covered lake surface. She raised one arm up in a jubilant, conquering gesture and let the sled coast out to almost the middle of the lake. I trudged out to my triumphant, courageous sister.

"What a solo flight, with a perfect five-point landing, prissy missy." I ran up to her, she stood and we gave each other a high-five. "Were you afraid?" I asked.

"Heck no, Justin. You think I am a baby or something? I want to do it again. Please, please, let's do it again."

"All right. Let me take my turn again and then you can make your encore performance. And then we need to go remind Gramps to come with us to the house and clean up before Mom and Kyle arrive."

"I don't like Kyle. He is strange," Christy blurted out. And I had to agree. Something about him was not right.

We slogged back up the hill for our second ski-jump thrill ride. This time I picked up enough speed that when I became airborne, I landed on the lake surface with such force that when I stuck out my leg for the drag effect, I spun around in a complete circle. Christy was at the top of the hill cheering me on again.

I made the last trip back up to the top of what now seemed like a mountain, got Christy situated on the sled again and ran down to stand next to the ski-jump. Down she came with no toe drag, too fast, I worried, and hit the jump-bump and sailed like a butterfly through the air to land perfectly on the lake surface and cruise out to the middle again. I raced out to her and we did another high-five for my happy camper.

"Give me a ride back to the house. Please, Justin, I'm tired," she smiled up at me.

"Okay, climb on board." I started to pull the sled rope, guiding us back towards the house. Man, not only was she getting older, she was getting heavier to pull every winter. Pretty soon, she'd be pulling me.

"I have a new name to remember today," she said.

"What is the new name, Christy?"

"Angel Flight, 'cause now I can fly like an angel." She started singing one of her school songs. Yup, she was my little angel sister—at least for a few more years.

CHAPTER 11

"Justin and Christy, your mom is pulling up in the front yard driveway. Are you both cleaned up from your sledding for dinner?" Grams asked. I clamored down the stairs almost bumping into Christy coming out of the bathroom next to the stairwell.

"You ready to see Mom and say hello again to your new stepdad-to-be?" I asked.

"I missed Mommy, but I don't like Kyle. He makes me afraid. Why is she marrying him anyway?"

"I don't know for sure. Guess he's the best meal ticket she can snag at this time."

"What's a meal ticket? And doesn't snag mean like someone catching a fish?"

"Yeah, something like that," I said. "Only snag means you're trolling the mucky bottom of the lake and you happen to snag, hook by accident, a dead turtle or an old log and you pull it up to the boat. At first, you thought you had a prize fish, only to discover you snagged a dead turtle, old log, you know, a piece

83

of crap. That's like what our mom is doing now." I laughed out loud.

"I don't understand your story, Justin," she replied.

"Forget it, prissy missy—bad joke. But in a few more years, you'll get it."

"Everyone, be nice now. We haven't seen your mom in a couple months and today is Thanksgiving. Be thankful." Grams heard us while hovering in the background. She opened the front door to greet Mom and Kyle.

"Well, hello Mom, love you, missed you. And how are my wonderful kids? Missed everyone so much." After hugging Grams, Mom came over to give Christy a big hug and kiss, and then grabbed my hand and gave me a peck on the forehead.

"And of course, you all remember Kyle." He stepped through the door entry, gave Gram and Christy a hug and shook my hand. And I noticed again his big hands. Then Gramps appeared at the door just behind Mom and Kyle and he went through the greeting routine with them.

"I hope you had a safe, easy trip," said Grams. "Hang up your coats, kick off your snow boots and come relax in the family room. Dinner is almost ready and I have some warm apple cider and crackers to tide us over 'til we eat. Barbara dear, your sisters and your brother are spending the day with their relatives, so they won't be joining us for dinner. Oh, your brother might be here later. So, it's only us and we'll have a wonderful time." Gram was bubbly and positive as usual. We all walked back into the family room, sat down on thread-bare couches and side-chairs while Gram exited to the kitchen to retrieve the cider and crackers.

"So, Justin and Christy, how has school been going—getting those straight A's? Both of my kids are smart as whips," Mom said to Kyle, reaching for his hand.

I smiled at her, trying to appreciate the sudden concern about our school and grades when in the last few months, nothing about the subject was mentioned in her limited and brief phone calls and letters. She sat there in her striking blue-and-white skirt and festive ski sweater, tailored to her slender frame. Her blond hair was loosely curled around her pretty face, with smooth, ivory skin, hazel eyes and Hollywood makeup. Yes, my mom was a showstopper and could get any guy she wanted. So, why this Kyle guy?

I glanced over at Kyle and noted his large six foot-plus frame, with long arms and those large hands. He was an average-looking guy with brown hair, hazel eyes, thin lips and crooked nose, dressed in jeans and a red-and-green checkered shirt. I heard he worked in some kind of office and didn't make much money. And he had the personality of a dead fish. This was the best meal ticket she could find? *Come on, Mom,* I thought. *Dad died six years ago and all the boyfriends you've gone through, you can do better than this.* But there was the extra complication of the rumor circulating around town. And Mom's extended stomach verified it…she was pregnant.

I looked over at Christy and listened to her ramble on about school, her friends and how we raced the sled down the ski-jump hill. We sipped the warm apple cider as Gramps and Kyle talked about ice fishing and the deer hunting season. Christy was bouncing her legs up and down sitting in a side chair, beginning to look bored.

"Okay, my dears, dinner is served and everyone please come to the table," Grams announced. We got up, walked into the front room and sat down at the dining table laden with a large, roasted turkey, mashed potatoes and gravy, cranberry sauce, homemade biscuits, venison dressing and corn-on-the-cob. I sat next to Christy and helped her pile up her plate while Gramps cut up the turkey with his extra sharp hunting knife. For a few moments in time, it was a pleasant and delicious Thanksgiving dinner. Then it all changed with Mom's comments about moving to the Cities.

"Well, my sweet children, are you getting excited about moving to the Cities right after Christmas? Kyle and I are going to rent a nice house out in Robbinsdale. I hear the schools are really good out there and you'll make lots of new friends," Mom droned on.

"What about all my cousins? Can they visit us when we move?" Christy asked.

"Of course, Christy. All your little cousins can visit us at any time. And you'll have your own bedroom and lots of new Christmas toys. It won't be much different from what you are doing now, even better," Mom continued the sales pitch.

"Do they have a hill where me and Justin can go ski jump with the Ryder sled?"

"No, not many hills around the Cities, I'm afraid," Kyle interjected. "Fact is, it's plain flat with a lot of big lakes. About as flat as the state of Kansas." He started laughing at his own, not-funny joke. Christy looked at me and scowled.

"Can Gramma come down and cook our meals sometimes?" Christy asked. I don't know if little sister realized it was a two-hundred mile, five-hour drive, one way.

"Darling, you know Mommy will be cooking your meals when I'm not working at the restaurant and we'll have pizza two or three times a week and I'll bring food home from

Charlie's Café. I know you'll miss Gram's cooking, but you'll get used to the new routine and love our home. Right, Justin?" Mom gave me that, be supportive, come-to-my-assistance look as she nodded her head in my direction.

"Yeah, Christy, it will be like eating special food at summer camp, only all year long. Remember how you liked church camp last summer?"

"I got sick and threw up for two days last summer camp." Christy looked down at her shoes and everyone got quiet at the table. I was struggling to keep a huge belly laugh from escaping.

"I'm sure everything will work out for the best. Dad and I will sure miss our grandkids living with us all these years," Grams said. She started making Christmas plans with Mom while Gramps and Kyle debated politics. Christy and I finished up our meal.

"Let me take the food into the kitchen and maybe, Barb, you can help me," Grams announced. She and Mom got up, cleared the meal and plates while Christy asked me if we could go sledding again. I squeezed her hand and told her maybe, watching her face light up. Then Grams set her famous dessert on the table; her strawberry-rhubarb pie with homemade vanilla ice cream. I became hungry again.

Everyone was finishing up with their fresh coffee. Christy and I excused ourselves from the table. I motioned for her to follow me to the kitchen storage shed where we pulled on our heavy jackets, boots and gloves and stomped outside into the glaring white, snow-covered backyard. The sun was dipping down over the pine tree tops, limiting our remaining sled runs.

We took my Ryder sled out from the outside storage shed and trudged towards our ski-jump hill. Soon, we were at the top again with Christy begging me to let her go first. I agreed, only with her assurance she would take it slow on the first run.

She positioned herself on top of the sled and I nudged her over the crest of the hill. I watched her race down the hill, hit the jump-bump and become airborne. I crossed my fingers as she sailed through the air, and then touched down on the snow-packed lake surface…a perfect landing. She let out a high-pitched squeal coasting the Ryder to the middle of the lake. She was becoming a pro at this ski-jump challenge. I slogged down the hill and helped her bring the sled to the top. It was getting dark and we would only have time for a couple more runs and then call it a day.

I took my run and let Christy take one more and then we headed back to the house. We put the sled back into the storage shed and were going up to the back door when she started crying.

"What is it, little miss?" I bent down and took her in my arms.

"I don't want to move away from Grams to the Cities," she sniffled in response. "I will miss all my cousins visiting and all my friends at school and…," she stuttered. "And I don't like Kyle. He has mean-looking eyes."

"Christy, I understand you don't want this move, this change, but remember, Mom let us live here because after Dad died in the car accident, she couldn't handle all her sorrows and the pressures of raising us. She had to go into that special hospital for a couple years and we were only going to be here temporarily. And now that she is all better and gonna get married, we have to move with her to the Cities." I looked into my sister's eyes, pleading for acceptance of my argument. But in the back of my mind, I was also concerned about the move and how it would affect Eric and our detective work on Randy's murder. And I was worried about this Kyle guy too. I couldn't put my finger on it, but like what Christy felt, he and his big hands made me uncomfortable. I hugged my little sister while she wept a few more tears. We went up to the house.

" 'Bout time you two got back. We were ready to send the game warden out looking for you," Gramps said between puffs off his cigarette. Everyone had returned to the family room.

"Justin, your uncle Stanley is coming down soon for some dessert and all the adults are going to play some penny-ante poker. You and Christy can watch TV and play games in the family room," Grams said.

I nodded my head in agreement, pulled on Christy's sleeve to follow me into the family room where we flicked on the old TV displaying a snow-patterned, barely visible rerun comedy. Christy pulled out a couple board games just as Uncle Stanley pushed his way through the front door, the noisy entrance announcing his arrival.

"Hello, son, glad you could make it," Gramps said. "You remember Kyle, Barbara's future husband."

Stanley acknowledged everyone, shook Kyle's hand, hugged Grams and nodded his head towards me and Christy.

I was glad the creep didn't come into the family room to shake my hand—would have refused. I watched him sit down, blather on about his successful hunting trips this season and slobber all over Gram's pie and ice cream. He glanced over at me and I know he picked up on the hatred reflected back from my eyes as the word "murderer" bounced around in my head. Here was one of cousin Randy's killers, a fucking murderer, welcomed to Gram's table. I almost puked.

"Justin, your move. Better hurry up 'cause I'm gonna beat you to home. Justin, are you OK?"

"Yes, prissy missy, everything is wonderful," I replied, getting back to our game.

"Let's bring out the cards. Time for a serious poker game," Gramps announced. "And bring out the cold beer we have in the fridge, Momma."

"Go easy on the beers. I don't want to see anyone get drunk tonight," Grams said.

"Don't worry, Momma, just a few beers amongst friends, right?" Gramps slapped Uncle Stanley on the back. Soon the cards, poker chips, dollar bills and cold beers were placed on the table and I noticed Mom's eyes light up. I said a little prayer that Mom would not drink too much and turn into that other horrible person. That person who drank herself into an alcoholic rehab facility for three years after Dad died. And that person who became violent when she got drunk. She was still fighting the demon, and since meeting Kyle in a bar several months ago, along with his excessive drinking, she had me worried. I had an uneasy feeling about tonight.

"Justin, you are not paying attention to our game so let's play another one." Christy folded up the board game and pulled down the Monopoly.

"It's almost eight-thirty and bedtime soon. One more game and then you need to hit the hay."

She yawned back at me as we set up the game. I knew she was worn out from the sledding excursion. Plus, I did not want her around downstairs while everyone got drunker and drunker.

She soon grew tired of Monopoly and started yawning again. It was now past nine-thirty when I told her it was time to hang it up and go to bed. We walked into the dining room where she said good-night to everyone, and then headed up to her bedroom. I whispered to her about brushing her teeth and not to worry about the move.

I made my way back to the family room counting over a dozen empty beer cans on the kitchen counter with another twelve-pack on the poker table. Sitting down on the couch, I watched Kyle pull out a small leather-covered container for liquor from his pocket and pour some hard stuff into his beer can and into Mom's. Oh no, now it had begun. Their speech was starting to slur and they didn't seem to care if they were losing at poker. They were both getting very drunk; Mom was getting loud and obnoxious and I was getting worried.

I busied myself reading through an encyclopedia section on the solar system, while listening to Grams trying to get everyone to end the drinking. She left the table and announced she would percolate some black coffee for everyone. Mom talked about how much she hated her job and the owner of the café and then launched into a long joke about one of Kyle's sisters. She went on ad nauseam, laughing about how stupid and retarded the sister was. Kyle laughed with her at first, but the more Mom carried on about his sister's IQ level, the more it began to bother him...I could see it in his eyes. I kept hoping Mom would tone it down, but knew it was way beyond that point. She was on a roll. And this was what Christy and I had to look forward to after moving with them to the Cities? But it was getting late, almost midnight now, and I was growing weary of listening to drunks talking about nonsensical issues.

Now Mom was going on, almost yelling, about how stupid Kyle's job was and that he should make more money. Then, she jumped back into the verbal attack on Kyle's sister and how Mom did not want the woman around her children. Grams came over to the table and told Mom to calm down, stop drinking and end the poker game. I glanced over at Kyle's face and noticed the veins popping out on his neck. I could tell he was growing angrier at Mom's verbal tirade.

"The coffee is almost finished so everyone can take a break and have a delicious cup with some of my homemade cinnamon rolls," Grams announced.

"And make sure Barbara gets several cups of coffee. She has had way too much to drink and her big, fat mouth has run away with her," Kyle almost shouted.

"Don't tell me I've had too much to drink," Mom replied, jabbing her finger towards Kyle's face. "I drink next to nothing, compared to that weird sister of yours. She is a drunken bitch every time we visit her house. She drinks twice as much as me."

No, no, Mom, calm down. You're going over the top. I was more nervous now, knowing she was exhibiting the dark side of her personality and would become more belligerent by the minute.

"Just shut your foul mouth for the next few minutes and everyone will be better off," Kyle replied. He put his large hand over her mouth and then it happened.

Mom pushed his hand away from her mouth and with her other hand, took a full can of beer and poured it over Kyle's head. He jerked his hand into the air and slapped the beer can away, sending it cascading across the table and onto the floor. With that, Mom got pissed and slapped his face, full force, with her open hand. Kyle locked her wrist in his hand and twisted it towards the floor, causing Mom to scream out in pain.

"Stop it! Stop this instant!" Grams was hovering over them, yelling. No good. It was too late.

Mom shot her other hand to Kyle's face and clawed his cheek, sinking her sharp fingernails into his flesh. Kyle grabbed

92

both her hands, lifted her out of the chair and flung her down on her back, onto the floor. Grams was screaming and while Uncle Stanley stood there stupefied, Gramps was trying to pull Kyle off Mom. I jumped up and rushed over to the melee and tried to help.

"Bitch, you bitch! You need to learn to keep your mouth shut." He put his huge hands around Mom's neck and started squeezing. Mom was gasping for breath and her eyes were rolling up in her head. Kyle was not letting go. I started pounding on Kyle's back and screaming for him to let Mom loose. He released his hands from around Mom's neck for a few seconds, pushed Gramps back and swung at me, knocking me to the floor. With blurred vision, I watched him resume choking Mom and thought he was really going to strangle her to death. I staggered back up and stumbled towards this unreal, bad dream scenario. Grams got there first and with a huge cast iron frying pan in her hands, brought it crashing down on Kyle's head. His eyes rolled back in his head and he tumbled onto the floor, releasing his death grip on Mom's neck. He groaned in a semi-conscious state, holding his head. Mom stood up crying, held by Grams. Deep, red marks encircled her neck.

"I hate you, you son-of-a-bitch," Mom yelled at Kyle on the floor. "Get the hell out of here. Get the hell out. It's over. I don't want to see you again." She was crying and screaming at the same time. I rushed over to hold her.

"Gonna kill you, you stupid bitch." Kyle rose back up and with his six foot-plus frame advanced towards Mom again.

"Time for you to leave our home…now." Gramps had a twelve-gauge shotgun pointed at Kyle's head. He unlocked the safety and cocked the gun, placed his finger on the trigger mechanism. Kyle stopped cold, evaluated the situation and pushed his hands forward, palms down.

"Come on, Dad, only kidding around with your daughter here. We argue and fight like this all the time," Kyle muttered.

"Damn liar. You never tried to strangle me before. You're crazy, just like your sister. Get the hell out of here. We're through. Never want to see you again." Mom broke into sobs again.

"That's it, Kyle. It's final. My daughter wants you out—now!" Gramps shoved the shotgun towards Kyle's face.

"Okay, I'm gone. Driving back to the Cities. Barb, we'll talk about this when you come back down and we're both sober." He turned around, marched to the front of the living room, reached for his jacket and boots and slammed the front door behind him. Grams and I held onto Mom while she continued crying.

"Has he ever done this before?" Grams asked.

"He has a temper, got into a fight with his crazy sister once at their place. I saw him hit her, but never thought he do something to me," Mom blurted.

"He had the look of a mad man in his eyes, daughter," Gramps said. "If momma had not hit him with that frying pan, don't know. I might've had to kill him with the shotgun."

It got real quiet in the room except for Mom's sniffling. Then Christy came walking over to us, rubbing her eyes.

"Mommy, what happened? I heard loud screaming and swear words."

I reached over and pulled my little sister into the family huddle. Mom was still weeping.

"Everything is all right, prissy missy. A little misunderstanding, that's all," I soothed. We heard Kyle race the engine of his car, put the car in gear and spin out over the snow-covered driveway onto the highway.

"Well, he's gone and good riddance," said Grams. "You're not going back to him, are you, Barbara?"

"No, I'm afraid it's over." Mom reached down and pulled off her engagement ring. "Would you like a nice, new diamond ring, Christy? Keep it locked away safe, for about twenty years."

"Wow. Of course. Thanks, Mommy, but why are you giving it to me?"

"Been a slight change of plans, sweetheart."

"A change of plans. Does that mean we're not moving to the Cities anymore?"

"Probably, probably yes. You and Justine are not moving to the Cities for now. As long as Mom and Dad can handle you a little while longer. But, next year, sometime, you'll be moving."

"Yippee! Hooray!" Christy yelled and clamped her arms around Mom's swollen neck.

I gave them both a hug and smiled to myself.

CHAPTER 12

It was a perfect Saturday morning after Thanksgiving. Christy was playing a board game with Mom in the family room, Grams was singing one of her church songs while preparing fresh homemade bread in the kitchen and Gramps was at the table, puffing away on his cigarette, repairing his fishing reel. I was sitting in the front room, staring out the window, waiting for Eric and his granddad to pick me up for our trip into Park Rapids. I couldn't believe it. Today we would drive over to Aunt Janet's house and meet up with Robyn and Audrey. My heart began racing so fast, I thought it was going to pop out of my chest. I was going to see my Audrey again, almost four months after her mysterious disappearance.

I turned to watch Mom laughing with Christy as they played their game. I was still stunned thinking about the recent turn of events with Kyle. It seemed like a bad dream, but Mom was emphatic in her promise never to get back together with Kyle the strangler. Of course I was happy we would not be moving to the Cities in January, but sad for Mom that another relationship went down the drain. Even though I missed Dad every day, I could never comprehend the deep pain and agony in Mom's heart after his death in the car/train accident. Even after all these years, I knew, because they were so much in love, the sorrow and hurt in her soul would never heal. And in her desperation to find someone to replace Dad, she continued to snag losers like this Kyle jerk. I watched her rub her expanding tummy and worried about our new brother or sister, due to arrive into our crazy family in a few months.

"They're here, everyone. Remember, I'm staying at Eric's place tonight and will be back tomorrow afternoon." Christy ran over to give me a hug and Mom blew a kiss in my direction. Gramps grunted some remark and Grams reminded me to be careful. I pulled on my snow boots over my shoes, slipped on my light-weight jacket, grabbed my backpack, patted Christy's blond ringlets and pushed through the front door and out into the brilliant-white winter day. I glanced up to see Eric waving at me, standing beside the luxurious Lincoln parked in the front yard.

"Little brother, long time no halitosis sharing," he laughed. We exchanged the high-five greeting. He took my backpack, tossed it into the open trunk, slammed the trunk shut and shouted a Geronimo as we clambered into the back seat. I said hello to Mr. Hodson as he pulled the car onto the highway towards Aunt Janet's place.

"You're staying with some relatives in town, Eric?"

"Yes sir, one of Gram's sisters' place. We'll be sleeping in the front room, me on a nice soft sofa bed and you in a sleeping bag. Not great, but it'll work for now. Take a look at these photos, Mr. Break-in, bad boy detective." He pulled out our latest black-and-white forensic fantastics. I flipped through the pictures, checking out the detail of the Nickelson Brother's overturned snow boot showing the gouged-out mark in the heel, with the dated file box in the background.

"I called Sheriff Copper and even though his office is closed today, he agreed to meet us there and we will turn over these pics to him. Another piece of evidence in place so we can nail the brothers' asses to the wall."

"These are so cool, Eric, but the way we got them, breaking in. Do you think the sheriff can use these in a court case?"

"It's all right. Sheriff told me over the phone, he can go to the judge and say he has information on probable cause, reason to ask for a search warrant. Anyway, when the sheriff sees these photos, he'll get the warrant, go down to the Kitty Lounge storage shed, take the boot evidence and arrest those murdering creeps."

"Sounds like a plan. But what about that stripper we saw on the street? You know, the one with the weird face? We gonna say anything about her?" I started humming the theme song from our favorite Sci-fi TV program.

"Justin, know what? After seeing that other stripper with her tits flopping out in front of us, with the big nipples and all, I think we were suffering from severe testosterone overload and it affected our vision, enhanced our imagination. What say we forget the lizard girl? Give me another high-five." He laughed again as I slapped his hand and said he was probably right.

We talked about how school was going for each of us and then got into detailed plans for the day. We would drop off the photos at the sheriff's office in Park Rapids and then drive out to Aunt Janet's and pick up Robyn and Audrey. I brought some of the cash from our giant fish pictures-for-money deal and told Eric that today was on me. We would take our ladies to the Saturday matinee and then to Taylor's for burgers and malts.

We would end our evening at Eric's place. It all sounded almost too good to be true.

"Here we are, boys. The sheriff's office is coming up, end of the block. Looks like his car is out front." Eric's granddad pulled into a parking space as we jumped out of the car, went up to the front door and entered the office.

"Come on back to my private domain, boys," the sheriff called out to us. "My deputy is off today and while waiting for you, I have been reviewing this file." We shuffled back to his private office, where he stood up to shake our hands and then motioned us to sit in a couple chairs in front of his desk. He quizzed us about school, any new girlfriends and then assumed a serious expression, looking at us from across the top of his large, folded hands. I was impressed once again with his football linebacker-like frame, shaved head, dark intense eyes and his tailored professional, pressed uniform confirming he was a no-nonsense, all-business police officer. He asked for the photos.

"I'm not going to inquire how you got these pictures and off the record, I don't even want to know. Now let me compare your photos to the pictures our office took of the boot imprints in the snow, at Randy's murder scene." He pulled out the crime scene photos and laid them next to our pictures of the gouged-out boot in the shed at the Kitty lounge. He smiled and nodded his head.

"Well, junior detectives, take a look." He rotated the paired photos around for us to see. Eric punched me in the shoulder. The boot print from both sets of pictures was a perfect match.

"So, sheriff, what's the next step?" I asked.

He gathered up the two sets of photos and stuffed them into two different envelopes then placed everything back into Randy's file.

"I pay a visit to my good friend, Judge Lansford, discuss probable cause and acquire a search warrant of the brothers' Kitty Lounge. I get said warrant, do the search, retrieve the boots in question and then meet with our local prosecuting attorney. At that point we'll decide if we have a strong enough case to charge the brothers in Randy's death.

"And you also have Gusta's testimony that the brothers were involved in Randy's murder and one of them actually pulled the trigger of a rifle that killed him," Eric added.

"You got it right, my boy. We now may have a strong case here. We'll see. However, it's a holiday weekend and I need to get back to the family. And it smells like, from your hair and after shave, you fellas have plans for a Saturday afternoon that might include a couple of young ladies. Don't let me keep you from something more important than us reviewing the contingencies of this case." He smiled, stood up, and shook our hands.

"Yes, we do have plans today. We are meeting some special friends we haven't seen since the end of summer," I replied. We turned to leave his office and went back through his front door.

The sheriff followed us outside and then hesitated.

"Have a good time today, guys, and stay safe. One more item of news I debated whether to tell you. You do know, Gusta escaped from the juvenile detention center a couple weeks ago and I have suspicions he is staying at or around his pa's place on Pickerel Lake. I'd be extra careful if I were you."

Eric and I both stopped in our tracks, turned and stared back at the sheriff.

"No, we didn't know that, sheriff, and appreciate the warning, but we'll be Okay. Thanks again," Eric responded. We turned and headed to the car where we climbed into the back seat.

"How'd it go?" Eric's granddad asked.

"As usual, good news and bad news," Eric replied. "Good news is more evidence is now on the table to bring the guilty to justice. And the other news is one of the bad guys is out of prison and loose like a goose. But today, we are not going to worry about that and instead concentrate on spending a beautiful day with our ladies. Right, little brother?"

We gave each other high-fives and I laughed along with Eric. But deep inside, I was a little worried.

CHAPTER 13

We pulled into the front yard of Aunt Janet's place and had just enough time to get out of the car when the two most beautiful girls in the world came running out to greet us. Robyn was faster as she blurted out a quick hello to me and flew into Eric's arms. I watched as they hugged and kissed then turned around to see Audrey coming towards me with that fantastic smile. She stopped in front of me and I hesitated for an uncertain moment. Then, we fell into each other's arms for the most delicious hug of my entire life. She kissed me on the cheek and then we kissed each other soft on the lips. When we stepped back, holding hands, I heard her stifle a muted sob and I pulled her close to me again, offering what comfort and emotional support I could.

"Justin, it is so wonderful to see you again. I thought for awhile we might never get back together again. Please forgive me; lots of memories from last summer came flooding into my heart a moment ago."

"Every day I thought of you, wondering about your situation. Can't believe you're really here," I returned

"All right, you two, I know it seems like forever since you last saw each other, but it's only a few months. Come here, my favorite cousin, and give me a kiss."

Robyn gave me a warm hug and then planted a full-on kiss on my lips while Audrey gave Eric a special hug. Then the four of us held on to each other in a friendship circle. When we let go, Audrey was still a little choked up with emotion.

"Sorry, guys. Now that we are together again, all those memories from last summer with the swim parties at Pickerel Lake, Randy's death and us moving away...difficult to contain myself right now," Audrey murmured.

"Audrey, don't apologize. After what the four of us went through together last summer, it's understandable. But today, we are going to make up for these past few months with an unbelievable day planned by our man Justin with a movie, burgers at Taylors and a party at my aunt's house here in PR," Eric announced.

"Sounds so neat! We're ready to go," said Robyn. "I did promise my mom and dad we'd be back by ten p.m. tonight. She's there on the porch now, kinda watching us."

We all turned, smiling, and waved to Aunt Janet as she waved back and reminded Robyn to be careful. We climbed into the large Lincoln with Robyn and Eric in the front seat next to Eric's granddad and me and Audrey sitting close in the back seat, all by ourselves. Perfect.

Eric and Robyn were talking up a storm in the front seat as Mr. Hodson tooled down the road towards PR and our date at the afternoon matinee. Audrey snuggled closer to me, both her hands clasped over mine.

"I cannot believe we are finally together again, Justin. You know how much I've dreamed about this? So, tell me everything. What is the latest on the giant fish and your detective work on Randy's murder? I so miss Randy and after what all of us went through last summer I still find it difficult to accept his death."

"I miss him, too. Eric and I are collecting more evidence on his case. But I wanted to hear your story first. Why did your family move away at the end of last summer, with no good-bye except a short note? And where are you living now? What is your dad doing with his secret government job concerning our monster fish in Pickerel Lake?"

"Okay, my sweet boyfriend. Can I call you that? Anyway, I'm sorry that when we moved out in the middle of the night, I could only leave you a brief note. You deserve to know why we had to leave."

I listened in fascination as Audrey relayed the story of the danger their family was in that necessitated their middle-of-the-night escape. She filled me in on the details concerning her father's secret information on the giant Pickerel Lake fish and talked about her current location near Duluth and her new distasteful school. And then came the best news, when she stated her family could be moving back to their house in PR next year. We gave each other another hug.

"All right, you two. Save it for the party tonight," Eric laughed back at us.

"Now it's your turn, my brave knight from Pickerel Lake. Update me on all the latest detective work."

I filled her in on the details of our adventure retrieving the boot photo evidence at the brothers' Kitty Lounge in the Cities and turning it all over to the sheriff …leaving out the part about the strange-faced stripper that passed us on the street.

"Did you and Eric get excited when you saw the stripper's breasts flop out in the open night air?" She asked, tickling me in the inquisition process.

"Eric got more excited than I did, I'm sure. But the main thing is we scored some great photo evidence, which we turned over to Sheriff Cooper. And then we got the bad news about Gusta escaping from the juvenile detention center."

"What? That really worries me, Justin. After all we went through with that creep scaring us at our party in your uncle's cabin and later stealing your money and attempting to shoot you. I thought it was over when he got sent to jail. Are you worried he may come after you for revenge?"

"It's possible, he might. But I know the sheriff is on his trail and I don't think he wants to be sent back to prison. My guess is Gusta believes his freedom is more important than revenge and has probably left the state."

"I hope you are right," Audrey answered. "After everything we've experienced with the giant fish, your cousin Randy's murder and the situation with your mom...you deserve better. Are you and your sister Christy still moving?"

"No, not now. That move has been postponed 'cause Mom and her fiancé broke-up this past week."

"Really? What happened?"

"Well, Mom doesn't want me to talk about it. I can only say their situation went from the frying pan into the fire and then everything hit the fan," I laughed.

"Understand, I guess. So, when my family moves back here next summer, you and Christy will still be at your grandparents' place at Pickerel Lake?"

"I hope so, Audrey." I leaned over to give her a kiss on the lips.

"Okay, you lovebirds. We're here at the matinee," Eric announced over the front seat.

Mr. Hodson pulled up into a parking spot and we exited his car.

"Thanks a bunch, Gramps," Eric said. "Pick us up about five at Taylor's." We waved good-bye to our chauffeur and meandered over to join the line of moviegoers in front of the theater. The marquee announced Abbott and Costello in "Africa Screams." Not my favorite type of movie, but the idea of sitting next to Audrey for almost two hours in a darkened theater, holding hands and snuggling…well, almost any movie would have been acceptable.

I paid for the tickets with a crisp twenty dollar bill. We got some popcorn and sodas at the concession stand and then ascended the plush carpeted stairway, up to the balcony section. We sat down in a secluded corner, above and away from the noisy, screaming kids on the main floor.

The movie was a predicable comedy with a few humorous scenes that Audrey seemed to enjoy. Between sharing the popcorn and sodas, I held her hand, laughing along with her at the comedic antics of the two crazy actors. I leaned over to whisper how happy I felt to be with her again. She placed her finger under my chin, turned my face to hers, kissed me on the lips and whispered, "Me, too."

I glanced over at Eric and Robyn, listening to their whispering and subdued laugher. All too soon, the movie was over, the theater lights came back on and the giant, red patterned curtains closed across the movie screen. We stood up, watched the wild mass of kids below us exit and descended the balcony steps to the lobby below.

"What did you think of the movie, Eric?" Audrey asked.

"What movie?" he replied. "Me and Robyn were putting together our own action production." I punched his shoulder and Audrey wagged her finger at them commenting something about them being naughty. We all laughed together again.

"Anyone hungry?" I asked. "Let's walk over to Taylor's and grab some burgers and malts." We followed the crowd out of the theater, crossed the street and turned left towards PR's favorite teen hangout.

The place was crowded when we arrived and we were lucky to get one of the last booths in the back. Old man Taylor with his small skinny frame, acne-pocked rodent-like face and high nasal voice was behind the counter shouting orders to his teenage short-order cook while instructing a new girl on how to make malts. He glanced in our direction with a weird, what-are-you-doing-here look, his eyes following us to our booth.

I nodded to Eric while memories of our last visit here at Taylor's with the Nickelson brothers flooded into my mind. Randy's murder, the exchange of the giant fish photos for cash, the involvement of Gusta with the Nickelson brothers all seemed like it happened just yesterday. I looked around, absorbing the atmosphere of this landmark malt shop with its red-and-white striped booths, bar stools and the candy-striped uniforms of the waitresses. Large photos of teen rock singers covered the walls with their music blaring from the oversize jukebox sitting at the back wall next to our booth. A couple girls from school walked past us, waving and giggling their way to the front of the shop.

"Eyes front, sailor. Don't stare too long at those pretty girls," Audrey teased me while tickling my ribs. I remarked that I only had eyes for her while we surveyed the menu. Everyone agreed on the standard fare of burgers, fries and chocolate malts, which I ordered from our cute, perky waitress. In minutes, she was back with our lunch.

"So Audrey, for sure your family gonna move back here next summer?" Eric asked.

"Well, I've got my fingers crossed and Mom is excited about getting our house back here in PR. But I worry about Dad chasing that giant fish in Pickerel Lake. I overheard a phone conversation with Dad reviewing a government plan to locate and capture the fish this next spring, after the ice melts."

"What? What's that about?" Eric asked between bites of his burger and slurping down his malt. "And wouldn't he be surprised to find out there are two fish, not one."

"Please, Eric, don't make it more complicated. We don't know that for sure. Anyway, while folding clothes in the laundry room, I heard Dad go on to review a plan to come back next spring with a couple large government boats, and track down and capture the monster fish."

Eric and I reached across the table giving each other a high-five while he let out a loud whoop and laugh.

"How they gonna do all that…with a thirty-foot rod and reel and a number fifty-size eagle claw hook?" Eric laughed. "Little brother, I would love to see this go down when they show up next spring. Audrey, on what date is your Dad gonna do all this?"

"I don't know, for sure. I thought I heard him mention a day in late April."

"Come on, Eric," Robyn replied. "You and Justin have done your part, with our expert help of course, and we got pretty close to the cutting edge of this adventure when your fish almost tipped over our boat. Remember? Relax and let Audrey's father and the government take care of the problem."

Robyn turned her face towards him and gave Eric a brief kiss on the lips.

"I know, I know. But this is so damn exciting. Wouldn't it be cool to hang around in the background, hiding in our boat behind some shoreline reeds, and take photos once they capture that fish or both fish?" Eric replied.

"Okay, Eric, it would be interesting. But today, let's concentrate on the here and now, celebrating our reunion with our lovely maidens," I said. "Three cheers to our perfect day." I held up my malt glass while everyone else raised their glass and we clanked them together.

"Speaking of the here and now, time to head over to my aunt's place for some real rock and roll music and later some food," Eric said. I turned over the check and left seven dollars to cover our lunch plus a generous tip for Trudy, since she was from my homeroom at school. We walked out the front door, with Mr. Taylor giving us the eye once again. Eric spotted his granddad driving towards us, up the street. Eric flagged him down and we scrambled inside the plush Lincoln.

"You kids having a good time?" he asked.

"The best, Mr. Hodson, and we so appreciate you chauffeuring us around today," Robyn replied.

"My pleasure. Only too happy to help you four enjoy your day together. We are now on our way to Momma's sister's place, just outside of town."

He turned a corner at the end of the block, connecting to a main county highway going south out of town. Eric said it was only a couple miles before we would arrive.

CHAPTER 14

We got out and stretched and I took Audrey's hand as we gazed across the expansive snow-covered dead stalks of the cornfields surrounding a two-story house with a guest house in the back. The sun was descending past the treetop line of the pine forests bordering the flat farmland encircling Eric's aunt's home. We followed Mr. Hodson to the front door of a gabled column, massive two-story, almost-new home.

"So wonderful to see special friends of Eric once again. The last time was at Justin's grandparents' for that end-of-summer barbeque," said Mrs. Hodson, greeting us at the entrance. "This is my sister Annabel."

Robyn and Audrey gave them both a hug and Eric and I shook everyone's hand, glancing around, noticing all the old, but expensive-looking antique furniture.

"Come in, my dears. I have some warm apple cider and homemade cookies," Annabel announced.

I could see we would spend most of this day eating.

We entered the living room, sat down and listened to the senior chatter between the sisters and Mr. Hodson. When

Annabel brought out the refreshments, we fielded questions about school, our families and activities with our friends. Annabel heard some of the rumors about the giant fish in Pickerel Lake and was fascinated when Robyn relayed a few more details about our photo adventure and encounter with the monster fish and how he almost capsized our boat. It was fun reliving our summer experience with these older, sweet people.

"The kids want to spend some time listening to their music and indulging in a pizza party later on, before I drive everyone home this evening. Gonna show them to the guest house in the back," Mr. Hodson said. "All right, gang, follow me. I think you will like your party house. I did order some pizza to be delivered in about an hour, plus Momma and Annabel are preparing a light dinner for tonight."

Yes sir, it was food day, all the way. We stood up, thanked Annabel for the snack and allowing us to use the guest facilities and followed Eric's granddad out the back kitchen door, down the walkway, to the guest house.

The house was painted an interesting muted sky blue color with yellow, red and white flower designs added around the door and window frames. There were garden decor ornaments attached to the sides of the roof following a front A-frame arch on both sides, almost touching the ground. It reminded me of a gingerbread house straight out of a child's storybook. I glanced over at Audrey; she squeezed my hand and winked back at me.

Mr. Hodson opened the front door, motioned us in and I was surprised to view an oversized front room with hardwood floors, a sofa and loveseat and a large jukebox off to the side. Adjoining the room was a kitchen and a dining area that included a round table and four side chairs. Unlike the furniture in the main house, this appeared modern and comfortable. A

112

hallway went off to the left connecting to what looked like a couple bedrooms and a bathroom.

"Kick off your shoes, get comfortable and enjoy yourself," announced Eric's grandpa. "Sodas and snacks are in the refrigerator. I set the wall temperature for seventy degrees, but you can adjust the thermostat to your liking. That is a working jukebox with about one hundred songs on it, mostly rock and roll with some country western. Hope you approve of the music. Best thing about it, doesn't need any nickels to work. You can select your favorite tune, with no pay…and play, all day long." We all cheered and applauded Mr. Hodson waxing poetic.

"Sounds like heaven to me," Eric said. He discarded his snow boots and motioned for Robyn to accompany him while they checked out the refrigerator. Audrey and I thanked Mr. Hodson for his hospitality.

"Least I could do for you kids, knowing what you went through with your cousin's murder, that wolf dog attacking you and Eric and that Gusta guy trying to kill you. You kids enjoy yourselves for a few hours and let me know if you need anything."

I shook his hand and Audrey gave him another hug.

He exited the front door with Robyn yelling thanks from across the room.

"Okay. We have the rest of the day to celebrate before gramps has to drive you ladies home later tonight," Eric said. He took some cola drinks out of the refrigerator while Robyn and Audrey ran and slid on their socks over the hardwood floors to the jukebox to survey the song selection. Soon there was a Rockin' Robin rendition blaring out over the speaker system and all four of us were out on the floor, dancing in our stocking feet.

Robyn and Audrey started performing their fancy rock and roll hip gyrations, looking sexier by the minute. I felt a little self-conscious, not knowing half the steps they did. Audrey took my hands and whispered not to worry, to just follow her lead.

I was amazed once again how being with her boosted my ego and self-confidence. I glanced over at Eric and Robyn rocking and laughing like dance competition champions.

We danced a few more fast rock songs and then the girls excused themselves to the bathroom to freshen up.

"Eric, this place is fantastic. So great that your aunt let us use this guest house."

"Yeah, she has some nieces and nephews come by and hang out here all the time. Her husband died a few years ago and left her a boatload of money. So, she remodeled this place, put in the jukebox and now it's teenage heaven."

The ladies returned. We retrieved our cola drinks and sat on the sofas, listening to more music. We talked about the good times we had last summer before Audrey and her family had to move.

"But enough of that. We're together again with some precious time granted us," Robyn said. "Hey, a beautiful slow song from my favorite singer, Ricky. Out on the floor, Eric." She stood up, pulled Eric into her arms and they strolled out on the dance floor.

Audrey gave me that special look and we also stood up and followed their lead.

The strains of the "Traveling Man" song drifted through the air as I held Audrey close to me, intoxicated by the aroma of her just-applied perfume and relishing her soft skin against my face. She turned her head towards me, staring deep into my eyes. We kissed and stopped dancing as she encircled her arms around the back of my neck. She opened her mouth, sliding her tongue over my front teeth. I responded in turn, hesitating at first and then exploring the possibilities of my first French kiss. I felt the room begin to spin.

"All right, you two. Save that till later," Eric scolded.

We ended our passionate kiss; I felt my face turning red and noticed Robyn pointing her finger at us, giggling. We sat back down on the sofa listening to another rocker song blasting when we heard a knock on the door.

"Pizza guy with your delivery." We rushed to the front door, jerked it open and almost knocked the poor kid over bringing in three boxes of pizza. I paid the bill, which included a generous tip, thanked him, dropped the pizzas on the table, refilled our soda drinks and dug into the most delicious pizza in the universe.

The rest of the afternoon flew by. We ate most of the pizzas, drank more cola and I was stuffed. Mr. Hodson dropped by later to inquire if we wanted dinner and we begged off, asking if we could spend the last hour or so in the guesthouse. Of course it was okay with him and he told us to enjoy ourselves.

I used the restroom and noted there were new guest toothbrushes and mouthwash. A nice touch and I took full advantage of it. I went back to the front room where everyone was laughing at one of Eric's jokes.

"Our turn," the girls announced. They jumped up and headed to the bathroom.

"Well, little brother, down to the last couple hours with our maidens. You having a good time?"

"The best, maybe the best in my life. Wish Randy and Marlene were here with us to enjoy it also."

"Think about next spring, Justin. Audrey promised to let me know when her dad will try to capture the giant fish, and we will be there. Same as last summer, the four of us, a picnic lunch, and the final answers to the Pickerel Lake mystery dedicated to Randy."

The girls came out of the bathroom, their hair reteased, new lipstick applied and a certain look in their eyes.

"Time for some romance," Robyn announced. "I'm spinning some mood music." She selected several tunes on the jukebox, walked over to turn off a couple lamps, and motioned Eric to her side.

"We are retiring to the bedroom," Robyn said. "Don't worry; nothing serious. Only gonna stretch out, get comfortable and share some stories in French. You two, enjoy yourselves on that soft, comfortable love sofa." She giggled and Eric gave me a high-five. They meandered down the hallway, turned into the bedroom, leaving the door open. I hoped Eric remembered my advice about Robyn's dad being super protective of his daughters. He promised me earlier the clothes would stay on.

Audrey gently pulled me down to the sofa next to her as a beautiful love song filled the air. She wrapped her arms around me and we started kissing again. Soon our tongues were touching and I was savoring her sweet, mouthwash-fresh saliva. She stretched out, positioned her body into the middle of the sofa and pulled me over on top of her.

"I'm falling in love with you, Justin. I never want to leave you. I am so happy."

"Audrey, I loved you from the first moment I saw you. You are so special; sometimes I feel I don't deserve you."

We continued to kiss, pressing our bodies together. The temperature in the room was rising. Audrey guided my face down towards her opened blouse and loosened her bra to expose part of her breast. I thought what was happening now related to all that stuff Eric and I laughed about in those girly magazines.

"I love you, Justin, and want you, but we need to wait, to be sure." She smiled up at me, running her fingers through my hair. We sat up on the sofa, both of us cooling down, and adjusted our loosened clothing. I struggled with my physical desires, these new emotions I never realized lay hidden deep inside. For a sheltered county boy, this was exhilarating, but like Eric said last summer, maybe I wasn't quite ready for prime time.

"We need to get back soon. Let's go disturb the love birds in the bedroom," Audrey said, pulling me up with her for a final embrace.

We tiptoed back to the open door of the bedroom and then jumped into the room, screaming a surprise. They were lying on the bed, talking, with Robyn fighting back tears. Thank God, their clothes were still on.

"What's wrong, Robyn?" Audrey sat down on the edge of the bed.

"Nothing. It's nothing. Today has been a special day and I'm going to miss my Eric so much." She put her arms around him and they kissed again. We heard a knock at the front door.

"Uh, oh, Gramps is here. Afraid it is time to hit the road." They arose from the bed, stood up and adjusted their clothes and hair.

"It's cool, guys. Gramps understands young love."

We headed back into the front room and let Mr. Hodson in. We straightened out the front room, put on our shoes and went out the door to the main house. We said good-bye to Mrs. Hodson, thanked Annabel for her hospitality, gathered up our jackets and exited the front door to climb into the Lincoln. We waved good-bye one more time. Audrey cuddled up with me in the back seat, squeezing me as Mr. Hodson tooled down the road back to Aunt Janet's place.

All too soon, we arrived and pulled up in the driveway, got out of the car and held each other while whispering our final good-byes. Aunt Janet was on the front poor, arms crossed, watching us.

"I will write you every week, Justin, and we'll call every weekend. Maybe my parents will drive back here to visit during Christmas." She was holding on tight, fighting back the tears. I was so choked up I couldn't even answer and was almost crying myself. One long kiss and we both knew it was time. Eric and Robyn came over, we group hugged, and repeated our mantra: 'One for all, and all for fun.' The girls turned away and went up to the front porch to greet Aunt Janet, who was now hovering. We waved goodbye and jumped into the back seat. As Mr. Hodson pulled away, I looked out the passenger window one last time, glimpsing Audrey waving to us.

"It's okay, little brother. Robyn and I are making plans for us to get together in April...soon as we find out about Audrey's dad doing his thing with the giant fish capture."

I smiled and nodded my head in agreement. Somehow, it would all work out for the best and the fabulous four would be together again this spring.

CHAPTER 15

I placed my hand on the pellet pistol secured to the leather holster looped onto my belt, bolstering my self-confidence as I moved closer to the mink trap. The sun was setting over the tall pine trees to my right, off the trail, and I would have to hurry, checking these last two traps. I tugged on the shoulder strap of the burlap bag containing the other mink I captured and killed at the South Inlet location. It had been a profitable day. If I could get one more mink and maybe a beaver pelt, I would make about thirty dollars towards my savings for Christmas. Things were looking up.

I approached the trap area and noticed the bait line, without the bait, dangling from an overhead branch over a bloodied snow patch on the ground. I squatted down, listening to tree branches snapping under the weight of melted snow freezing back into ice as the afternoon temperatures dropped. I focused my attention on the red-splotched snow patch, about five feet in front of me, waited for any movement in the snow-covered leaves underneath the blood-spotted snow surface. Mink are not only very difficult to trap, but are also cunning and vicious once caught in the bear claw trap. I heard stories telling that when one of my cousins bent down to look closer at a possible trapped mink hidden under some leaves, next thing he knew, the trapped mink exploded out of the leaves and slashed a long claw mark down his cheek. Yes siree, with their long claws, sharp pointed teeth and aggressive nature...they were the most dangerous and formidable two-pound creature here in the forests of northern Minnesota.

I waited and watched in silence and then noticed a couple leaves in the targeted area move. Yup. He was hiding under the crusted snow cover, probably chewing his trapped leg off to escape, waiting for his opportunity. I picked up a loose twig and tossed it onto the blood-spot in front of me. Almost in an instant, the snow cover blew apart as the trapped mink leaped out of his protective burrow, snarling and hissing in my direction. I stood up watching him lunge towards me, dragging the trap and chain behind him. When he reached the two-foot limit of the chain, it snapped him back. I could see his one back foot, dangling by a few bloodied mangled tendons, inside the snapped shut jaws of the trap. Another hour or so and he would have chewed himself free and hobbled away, minus one foot, into the forest.

I pulled out my pellet pistol and circled around him. He continued to monitor my movements, facing me with his snarling, hissing and clawing attitude. I could try to find a smooth tree branch and hit him over the head for the final kill, but because of their speed and smaller head, that technique did not work as well as it did for gophers. So, the pistol was the most effective way to finish the job. I used to shoot them with a twenty-two pistol, but it made too big a hole in the head and even the body, ruining the pelt. Sometimes the bullet ricocheted off a rock in the ground. No, the pellet pistol was the most effective kill method and caused the least amount of damage to the fur pelt, as long as you got up close and were dead-on accurate. And I learned long ago the mink are vicious, but are not multi-tasked. The little brown creature with its white belly would be easy to distract.

I moved in closer now with a tree branch in my left hand and the cocked pellet pistol in my right. I pushed the branch forward, towards the mink, until it was close enough for him to reach out, grab it and pull it towards him with his vicious little front claws and sink his needle-pointed, razor sharp teeth into the bark. He was shaking it back and forth like a puppy, trying to dislodge it from my hands, his beady black eyes spewing hatred back at me. I pushed the twig into the ground, knowing he would not let go, and brought my pistol up to within inches of his head and pulled the trigger. The pellet, propelled by a super-charged CO_2 canister, smashed through his face, ripping away an eye and spewing blood and brain tissue out the back of his head. His jaw dropped open, releasing the twig, with almost a surprised look on his whiskered face, snarling one last time at me. I squeezed off two more quick shots, blowing away most of his remaining head. He collapsed to the ground, a fighter to the end.

I stood up, glanced down at my bloodied conquest, relieved it was over. But, I did not feel like the conquering hero staring down at my vanquished enemy. Instead, I was not proud of my role as a giant human being eliminating a little two-pound mink with a gun. The killing thing still bothered me. I released my dead adversary from the trap, opened the burlap bag and dropped him inside next to his dead companion. I would have to come back tomorrow with fresh chicken head bait, tie it to the dangling line just above a reset snow-covered claw trap. Strange how these mink were so smart but greed and hunger drove them to make mistakes...kind of like people. But, time to move on to my last stop; the beaver trap down by the lake.

I walked down the hill towards the large snow-covered beaver lodge at the edge of the shore. I could see the wooden stake next to the mound, plunged into the ring of the trap chain. It stood straight up and was not bent over, indicating there was no action on the trap. I approached the beaver mound with caution and jumped when hearing a loud slapping sound echoing from the lake. A watchful beaver had spotted me and slapped his flat tail onto the surface of the lake, warning his family and friends of an intruder in town. I smiled to myself. These forest animals were so intelligent and perceptive, so aware of their surroundings, it amazed me.

I walked up next to the beaver lodge, lifted up the chain and followed its length underneath the melted ice water to an entry hole into mound. I pulled the trap out of the water and noted the dead crappie still attached to the center spike device with the hinged steel jaws open. I placed the trap back into the water, positioning it near the mound opening. Oh well, another day maybe. Have to come back tomorrow and check it again. At least I had a couple minks and would make a few bucks. It was getting dark and I'd promised Grams I would be home before five o'clock. Time to head back.

I trudged back up the hill towards the edge of the forest and turned down a pathway towards the connecting gravel road that led to the house. I wasn't paying much attention to my surroundings, humming a song and kicking away some loose stones on the path in front of me. I glanced over to the left side of the pathway, careful of the steep embankment sloping down towards the lakeshore. I came around a clump of raspberry bushes and felt a rifle barrel jammed into my back.

"Well, cousin, long time, no see. What the hell you doing? Killing all those defenseless little animals for a few measly dollars?" I spun around, staring into the barrel of a 30-30 rifle leveled at me by Gusta.

"So it's true. You broke out of prison and now the whole state is looking for you."

"You got that right, Justin, cuz. And they could send cops from a dozen states searching for me and never get close. But that's another story. Anyway, life been treating you okay while mine has sucked these last few months?"

"Hey, man, you're the one who started everything. You should have gone to Sheriff Cooper, explained everything, when Randy first got killed."

"Yeah, yeah, don't lecture me, spoiled, protected Grandma's timid resort boy. Shoulda, coulda…it's all done now. In the meantime, you sent me to prison, where I almost got butt-fucked and killed the first week there. The way I see it, it's pay-back time."

I stepped back, beginning to run the possibilities of Gusta's threats through my mind. But I knew my options were limited to none.

"What're you talking about, Gusta? Judge sent you to reform school, not me. Only a couple years, you'll be out and can go back home, help your pa out on the ranch. Now you are blowing it."

"Okay, don't lecture me, you pathetic worm-digger. Get moving…I got a plan we need to…how you smart ass amateur detectives say it…activate?"

125

I cringed as Gusta jammed the rifle into my ribs, forcing me to turn around and walk forward on the trail towards the dirt road. Now what? Was he going to shoot me and make it look like a hunting accident?

"We're going on over to Uncle Stan's place and you're gonna tell him where you have the rest of that photo reward money hidden and he's gonna go get it and bring it back to us. I know you haven't spent too much of the original $500 you got from the Nickelson Brothers. And he's gonna bring all your skinned pelts from your storage shed and we're gonna sell them and split the proceeds. He's still pissed at you, cuz, thinking you tried to get him thrown in jail too. Anyway, I'm moving on to stay with some friends in the Dakotas and need some traveling money; figure you owe me. And if you cooperate, I promise not to kill you and only tie you up for awhile until I can be on my way. Don't know if Stan wants you around his place, though. May have to leave you tied to a tree out in the woods somewhere. Hope the wolves don't find you during the night and decide they need a snack. Guess at that point they would control the situation, because they control the environment. Right, Justin?" He laughed out loud as he continued to prod me forward with the rifle barrel.

What was I going to do? He could easily kill me once he got the money and the pelts. I said a quick prayer to the angels for help and guidance and wished Eric were here with me, wondering what he would do if in my position. It was getting darker and Stan's place was only another ten minutes down the trail. Then, without warning, I twisted my foot on some loose stones on the pathway, fell down and grabbed my ankle, grimacing in pain. Damn, what else could go wrong?

"Come on, lazy boy, quit faking and get on your feet." He lowered his gun for a moment, and reached down to pull me up. Moment of opportunity. I recalled the leg sweep move Eric had taught me this past summer. I gripped Gusta's hand, struggling to rise, when I pushed my strong leg out at Gusta's knee and then kicked my foot across the other leg. It caught him by surprise and he yelled in pain, crashing down on me. He dropped the rifle and I grabbed him in a bear hug as he tried to twist away from me. We slipped on the trail surface, fell down and together, rolled down the steep embankment, hurtling towards the lakeshore. Gusta was swearing at me as we clutched each other, rolling over and over across the surface of the snow. My glasses were gone, but I glanced up with blurry vision, spotting a group of tree stumps and large rocks jutting into view. We tumbled into them and I felt a heavy blow to my head and reeled into darkness.

CHAPTER 16

Gusta rolled up his pants leg, rotated his ankle and winced in agony as bolts of pain shot up his thigh. He felt around his right leg below the knee, examining a sensitive shin bone, wondering if his leg was broken. He glanced over at Justin, lying beside him with a bloodied knot on his forehead.

"Justin, wake up, man. Stop joking around and wake up." He reached over and shook him. He was limp to the touch, his eyes did not flicker and Gusta knew he was unconscious. "Right, you little ass wipe. I'm outta here and gonna leave you to the wolves." He struggled to stand and instead, collapsed into a heap of uselessness, pulling his legs up to his chest, in a fetus position, screaming with intense pain rocketing through his body. His right leg was broken and he was not going anywhere soon. He glanced out across the lake and watched the sun descend below the horizon, felt the temperature dropping. He thought he saw a pair of emerald green eyes staring at him from behind a group of pine trees, partway up the hill. Gusta and Justin's noisy arrival into this stump and rock ravine combined with the aroma of fresh blood from their wounds had set off the dinner bells for the local wolf community.

He brushed the snow away on the ground cover next to them, searching for his rifle and shouting cuss words into the darkening night air. Then he glanced up the steep embankment to the top of the hill and remembered, with terrified mental clarity, he had dropped his rifle when he and Justin struggled and rolled down the hill.

"Thanks a lot, you stupid fuck, idiot cuz. Now we are both going to die because of your weak, half-ass karate effort. Eric teach you that pitiful move? I was just gonna take some of your money, tie you up at Stan's place and take off for my friend's, out of your life forever. Now you think you're all brave and this is the result." He leaned over and punched Justin in the shoulder. He did not wake up.

Gusta struggled to his feet again, assisted by a thick tree limb he used as a makeshift crutch. He took a couple steps up the sloping hill and then collapsed again onto the ground screaming for the pain to stop. This was no good. He realized he was stuck here with the brainless boy.

He crawled back next to Justin and sat up to survey their situation. They were in a clump of tree stubs and rocks at the bottom of this hill, about one hundred feet from the lake. Off to the right and left were stands of pine trees intermixed with heavy shrubbery. The top of the hill was at least a couple hundred yards away. There was a half-cut log behind him, about twenty feet long and a foot in diameter, wedged between some large boulders, facing the lakeshore. There were cut pine branches, some of them dried out and the others still green, piled next to one end of the log. There were also a dozen or so smaller cut logs, about three feet long and eight to ten inches in diameter, stacked next to the log.

"Okay, Justin, you got any artillery on your person?" Gusta grimaced in pain as he crawled over next to his cousin, rolled him over and searched through his pockets. He found nothing except the pellet pistol encased in his side holster.

"Well, this will certainly do the job in keeping a dozen wolves at bay." He pulled the pistol out of the holster, fired off a couple rounds into the log next to them, laughed at the results then jammed the pistol back into the holster.

"That toy will never save anyone's life. Once again, the resort boy ventures into the wild totally unprepared." He reached down to his belt and felt the oversized Bowie hunting knife strapped to his good leg. Damn. Why wasn't he packing his twenty-two automatic pistol on this trip? He cursed himself for not being better prepared as he glanced up the embankment again; mentally willing his rifle to move to the edge of the trail and slide down the hill to their location. *Okay, Gusta*, he thought, *come back to the world of reality.*

He didn't have his watch on, but remembered Justin always wore his and turned over his wrist, noting it was almost five-thirty. He knew Justin's Gram would be worrying now that he wasn't home and would be sending Gramps out to look for him. They had to hang on for awhile and help would arrive. And then Gusta noticed a couple more sets of emerald green eyes, behind some trees to the right of their location. The eyes were moving closer to them and he realized they did not have much time.

"Got to build a fire, a huge fire with lots of smoke," Gusta announced. He rummaged through his jacket and pants pockets, searching for matches. Nothing. Always took matches with him into the woods, but not this time. He reached into Justin's pockets with the same zero results. Then he noticed the burlap bag strapped over Justin's shoulder. He snapped it open, taken aback by the pungent odor of the two dead mink carcasses in the bag. He noticed the pocket on the side of the bag, opened it up and found a compass, a Boy Scout knife and a pack of matches.

"Way to go, Justin. Always be prepared and all that other Boy Scout bullshit. It finally paid off and you made a good decision."

He pulled out the matches, stuck them in his pocket and crawled towards the end of the log. There was a stack of dried pine branches, which he gathered up, and edged his way back to Justin's side. He threw the branches on the ground, facing out towards the sloping hillside. Then, he pulled himself back and retrieved several smaller green tree limbs and dragged them over to the growing pile of branches. He returned one more time, loaded several three-foot logs into one arm and with his other arm, pushed himself along the ground back to the branch pile and muscled the logs onto the top of the pile. He pulled out the matches, lit several and tossed them into the pile of branches. It caught fire and erupted into a blaze, sending fire fingers into the sky. He glanced up at the pine tree stand to his right and was surprised to see four huge timber wolves, standing there, observing his actions, only about thirty yards away.

He picked up a couple rocks and tossed them at the stealth forms, watching them fall short of their mark. A couple wolves seemed to nod at each other and circled around to the front of the campfire. One of them raised his nose in the air, sniffing to determine if their potential meal was man or beast. One of them sat down on his haunches, licking and nipping at one of his legs near his shoulders, obviously dealing with a wood tic or itch. They looked back at Gusta as one raised his head in the air and emitted a mournful wolf cry. They were calling in enforcements and Gusta knew he and Justin were running out of time.

He took some wet leaves and snow and tossed them on the blazing fire, creating a giant smoke plume that curled into the cold night air. Maybe someone would notice the large smoke column and investigate. A half-moon was rising above the horizon, casting a faint glow upon their unfolding drama. Gusta heard some rustling noise off to his left now, and peered out to count a total of five wolves gathered for the buffet dinner. They were edging closer to the campfire. What was their plan? Would they wait for a few more buddies and then charge the campfire all at once, overwhelming them? Time for some proactive measures.

He selected some shorter tree limbs, some dry and some green, stuck their front portions into the burning campfire, and when the flames had ignited half the branch, lifted them up and heaved them towards the encircling wolf pack. He threw out five of them, watching them hit the ground and spew forth sparks and tongues of fire into the air. The wolves backed away from the fiery intrusion into their space, confused at this new roadblock hindering their forward movement. Yes! It was working.

Now he pulled on his extra pair of leather gloves, extracted a smoldering log and heaved it over his head towards the encircling beasts. The log smashed into the ground, exploding and sending sparks and debris into the air. He watched with satisfaction as the log rolled towards one of the wolves and he actually had to dance out of its way to escape from being hit. He pulled out three more logs, tossing them in different directions, away from the campfire. The wolves continued to back away, seeming still confused by this new development. A couple of them turned around and retreated into the safety of the pine trees and shrubbery.

"Assholes. You don't know who the fuck you're dealing with here," Gusta shouted into the night. But now he paused and counted the total wolf pack and realized it had grown to seven. The logs out on the perimeter were burning down and not that many more logs were left in the campfire. One of the wolves lay down on his haunches, stared directly at Gusta and opened his jaws in a wide, relaxing yawn. He seemed to be telling Gusta they would wait it out until the perimeter logs burned down, and then attack in full force.

He had to get more branches and logs into the fire. He shook Justin again with no response. He was still unconscious and Gusta knew it was all up to him with his broken leg. He dragged himself back to the pile of tree limbs, bundled together several with one arm and with the other arm, pushed himself over the snow surface to the fire and threw them into the blaze. Then he made a return trip for the logs, secured three with one arm and pushed back again to the campfire, thrusting them into the flames. He was getting tired, cold, and hungry and feeling his energy and strength ebbing. He glanced up, noticing one of the wolves smiling back at him while watching his futile efforts. He turned over Justin's wrist to check the time: almost six-thirty.

"God, help us, please send some help," he screamed into the night air, surprised at his sudden utterance. Should he, could he call on a God he didn't believe in, to help them in this situation and save him and, yes, even save his worthless cousin?

"God, please help us. I'm out of ideas and we are running out of time." Tears welled up in his eyes and he realized it was the first time, since his early days in prison, he had cried. Maybe he should have cried and prayed more often these past few years.

The wolves were on the move again, edging closer, developing their attack strategy. He reached for a couple burning branches and heaved them towards the encircling horde. They paused a moment, undeterred, stepped around the new obstructions and continued their march towards the men. A couple of the pack were now growling, ominous sounds reverberating in their throats. Their eyes seemed to glow with a brighter emerald green in anticipation of the kill.

Justin let out a moan and started to roll over.

"Come on, man, wake up and help me out," Gusta yelled. He bent down to prod Justin awake when a black form, hurling through the air, landed on Gusta's back, locking his jaws onto his jacket collar and ripping it apart with his back and forth head motions. Gusta reached up and with his muscular arms, pulled the wolf down on the ground and fell on top of him. The wolf was snapping and clawing at his face as Gusta locked his hands around the animal's throat, attempting to strangle him. The wolf was too strong and Gusta was losing this battle. Then he remembered the pellet pistol, and while holding the snapping jaws at bay with one arm, reached over with his free hand to Justin's limp form, pulled the gun out of the holster and jammed the barrel of the gun into the mouth and throat of his attacker. He held down the semi-automatic trigger, discharging a half-dozen pellets into the throat of the wolf. In the few moments when the wolf hesitated, Gusta pulled his Bowie knife from his belt and thrust it deep into the chest cavity of the wolf again and again, spilling his guts onto the ground. Gusta fell back, exhausted, towards Justin, while the wounded beast staggered to his feet, coughed up blood and collapsed into a bloodied mass of fur and twitching legs on the snow-covered ground. The other wolves were distracted for the moment and then began to storm across the clearing to their campfire. Gusta glanced up to see the charging horde and knew they were going to die.

A shot rang out and the lead wolf crumpled to the ground in a bloodied heap of fur and flesh. Two more high-caliber shots sang through the air and two more wolves crashed to the ground, their chests ripped apart by 30-30 rounds, exploding on impact. The other wolves stopped their advance on the campfire, hesitated at the sight and smell of their dead comrades and turned to vanish back into the pine trees and underbrush. Gusta looked up to see his pa and Justin's granddad scrambling down the hill towards their smoldering campfire. He hobbled to his feet and fell into the arms of his dad, fighting back the tears and uttering his first prayer of thanks since childhood. Justin's grandpa rushed over to Justin, knelt down, and wiped away the blood from his forehead. Justin was beginning to stir.

"Don't tell me what's going on here, Gusta, don't want to hear your lame story," Clive bellowed at his son.

"Come on, Clive. The boys are safe now. Let's get them back to the house," Justin's granddad ordered.

Gusta put his arm over the shoulder of his dad and with his assistance, turned to ascend the hill. He glanced back at the carnage of the dead wolves sprawled out next to the dying campfire, now comprehending just how close to death they'd come. Justin's granddad picked up the still semi-unconscious Justin in his strong arms and trudged up the hill to the trail at the top. Gusta listened to his pa going on and on about how stupid the boys were being out here at night with the hungry, vicious timber wolves. He smiled to himself as he found himself enjoying the sound of his dad's ranting.

CHAPTER 17

"Hurry up, Justin. Our cousins are getting out of the car and you promised."

"Okay, prissy, missy. I'm here. Let's go out and welcome them to our Christmas party." Christy squeezed my hand as she skipped alongside me up the walkway towards the front parking driveway. Most of the time she was a veritable social butterfly but when the cousins showed up, she needed me to go with her to greet them. I think it was their money and new cars that intimidated her. I looked up to see Aunt Janet waving at us while Robyn, Marlene and their younger brother and sister piled out of their fancy Cadillac sedan. Uncle Hal closed the driver's side door and bent down to wipe a speck off the gold-tone exterior. Christy let go of my hand and ran up to give her cousin Sarah a big hug. Nine-year-old Sarah with her bouncy, ash blond ringlets, pre-teen makeup, and very pretty, almost Hollywood child-star facial features, had already been in a couple commercials, her parents grooming her for stardom. She was dressed in her expensive snow pants and designer jacket. As she stood next to Christy in patched jeans and nylon windbreaker, I felt a little sorry for my sister. But, despite the disparity of social class, Sarah and Christy were like sisters and loved spending play time together. I watched them as they giggled and chattered away.

"Hello, cousin. In spite of that bump on your forehead, not quite healed, you look as yummy as ever." My face flushed as Robyn came up to me and gave me a warm hug and kiss on the cheek.

"My lovely maiden Robyn, beautiful and charming as ever." I returned the hug and then said hello and hugged Marlene and Aunt Janet. I shook Uncle Hal's hand and nodded acknowledgement to Robyn's younger brother who stood off to the side with his hands stuck in his pockets.

"Come on inside, everyone, Grams has some coffee, hot chocolate and fresh cinnamon rolls prepared," I said.

Robyn wrapped her arms around my arm as all of us walked down the pathway to the front porch.

"Hear anything from Audrey? Rumor has it she might be able to visit us sometime during the Christmas holiday," Robyn inquired.

"No, I talked with her on the phone a couple days ago and she said security was tight again about her dad traveling out of the area. So, she's not certain they can come down for a visit. Did say she sent me a letter. Hope it arrives this afternoon. We'll see. But Eric may be coming up with his grandparents for a couple days after Christmas. Course, you already knew that, Robyn."

"Yes, he mentioned something about that on the phone. I miss him gobs and gobs and kept thinking about the memorable party we had at his aunt's guest house in PR. That was such a blast."

We opened the front door into the living room with Grams and Gramps waiting to welcome their favorite daughter and family to the homestead. Grams ushered us into the kitchen where the table was laden with coffee, hot chocolate, cups, small plates and fresh, homemade cinnamon rolls. Robyn, Marlene and I filled cups with hot chocolate and I loaded up a plate with the rolls then together we all retreated into the sun-drenched family room.

"So, dear Justin, what Christmas activities do you have lined up for your favorite cousins?" Robyn asked, sipping her hot chocolate and sampling a cinnamon roll.

"Uncle Stan will be arriving soon with his wife and horde of kids. He is bringing a new set of snow skis and a racer-style, saucer sled. Said he will take us out on the lake, hook up the tow rope to his pickup truck and pull us around. You up for something like that?" I replied, finishing off a cinnamon roll and washing it down with some hot chocolate.

"Of course. Living dangerous is my middle name," Robyn replied.

"How 'bout you, Marlene? Ready for the thrill of a lifetime?"

"The lake is frozen thick, right? I mean, the car won't fall through the ice into the water or something? And he won't pull us too fast?"

"Marlene, Marlene. The lake is frozen over one foot thick. An eighteen-wheeler truck would not break through that ice. And with some fresh powder on the surface, it will be perfect for skiing or sledding and if you fall down, you will go sliding on a puffy snow surface." I smiled back at her, remembering how worried she was about every detail of our activities.

"Anyway, my mom will be arriving soon with a ton of presents she claims to have bought at the best stores in Minneapolis. Christy will get a lot of gifts from Santa."

"And your mom's boyfriend…will he be with her? Did they make up after that fight? And Justin, is your mom really pregnant?" Robyn leaned over to me, took both my hands in hers and waited for my response.

"No boyfriend, he is gone forever. She is totally depressed and I feel sorry for her. And yes, she is pregnant and hopes to have the baby even though the father is that particular boyfriend who tried to strangle her. Guess Christy and I will have a new brother or sister next April or so."

"How is your mom gonna take care of the new baby and work?" Marlene asked.

"Don't know, for sure. She might have to take some time off work and stay here at Grams for a couple of months with us helping out with the baby. Guess we'll see."

"And Justin, most important news of all: What really happened with you and Gusta out in the woods? We heard different stories and you didn't say too much on the phone," Robyn asked.

"Now that is a very interesting story. Let me fill you in on the details." I spent the next half-hour explaining our adventure in detail basing it on Gusta's version of the story and what Gramps told me later, since I was unconscious. Robyn and Marlene listened in rapt wonder.

"And what happened to Gusta? He had the broken leg. Did he go to his friend's house in Fargo?" asked Marlene.

"This part you are not going to believe…just happened in the past few days. After our wolf ordeal and rescue, he went to the hospital in PR where they put his leg in a cast, and his dad convinced him to turn himself in to Sheriff Cooper. He was held in a temporary cell and only two days ago, he went before the judge with his attorney and pled his case. I wrote a letter on his behalf that they read in court, explaining how Gusta saved our lives out there with the wolves. Anyway, given Gusta's new attitude, my letter and his father asking for mercy from the court, the judge reduced his sentence to six remaining months and transferred him to a half-way recovery house in Wadena. I think the wolf experience changed his attitude about life."

"Wow. That is great to hear. It will be interesting to see if he really changed when he comes back home, what...next June?"

"I think he is sincere, Robyn. We almost died out there in the forest with the attacking wolves. An experience like that tends to have an impact."

"So, back to Christmas. What else have you got planned, Justin?"

"Aunt Pauline will be here with her new boyfriend from college. She is going to teach us a new tag game on the ice she learned from college friends. It involves a giant circle drawn on the lake with cross passes connecting to the center and a strategy based on cat and mouse tag rules. Then she has some new Christmas songs she'll perform on the piano and have us all sing along like we've done every year. Grams is finishing a fantastic dinner and afterwards Santa will pay a visit to the kids and then we'll open about a thousand gifts. You have my present now, Robyn?"

"No, I don't, silly. Santa will bring it later." She punched me on the shoulder.

"Justin, girls...your uncle Stanley is here with Ann and the kids. Come say hello," Grams called out to us. "And Justin, the mail came and you have a letter from Audrey."

143

Robyn smiled at me and gave me a high-five as we strolled into the front room and went through the usual formalities. Uncle Stanley did not offer to shake my hand, but instead acknowledged my existence with a cold stare from across the room. It was all right…I couldn't stand him either. I hoped he didn't have a hidden agenda when he took us out on the lake for the ski and sled towing adventure. I snatched the letter off the table and motioned for Robyn to follow me back to the family room.

"Come on, I'll let you read it afterwards…if it's not too mushy." We bounced back into the family room and I tore open Audrey's letter.

"My dear Justin,

How I wish I could be with you this Christmas holiday.

Unfortunately there are continued security issues with my dad's job and according to him, we need to stay at our place for the holidays and cannot travel to PR. Give my love to Robyn, Marlene and Eric. I miss you all so much.

It won't be too bad. Some of mom's family will be visiting us and I'll spend time with a couple cousins I haven't seen in ages.

I was so terrified when I heard about your experience in the woods with Gusta and the wolves. I say a little prayer for you every day and know God's angels were watching over you, protecting you and saving you for me, only me. I miss you, miss you and want to kiss you, again and again. What are you doing to my tender heart?

I don't know, but guess what? You will have a chance to explain that to me because we will be visiting in the spring, around Easter. So, be prepared, young knight. Line up a party with Robyn and Eric for that time. Maybe a picnic at the lake again?

Say hello to everyone and have a wonderful Merry Christmas. Be safe and I will see you in my dreams.

Your first love, Audrey."

Wow! I felt a couple tears well up in my eyes as I handed the letter to Robyn.

"The party, the picnic is on for Easter," she screeched, reading through the letter.

"Justin, you call Eric and set it up with him and I will get the okay from mom. This picnic will be even better than the last one 'cause we don't have to take any fish pictures, right?" She gave me that quizzical look.

"Correcto. No fish pictures. This time Eric has a plan to capture the fish." I stopped and put my forehead up to hers, staring deep into her eyes and humming the theme song from the science fiction show on TV. She pushed me away with her famous giggle-scream.

"Justin, stop it, you bad, bad cousin. We are not going to capture any giant fish and in fact, we are going to leave him alone and he will not bother us…right?"

"Absolutely, my fair damsel. You have nothing to fear." She slapped me on the shoulder as we both started laughing.

"Justin, your mom is pulling up in the front driveway," Grams called out to me. I took the letter back from Robyn, folded it into my pocket and Robyn and I got up and hurried into the living room to welcome Mom to the homestead.

CHAPTER 18

"Let's get a move-on, Justin. Round up the kids while I hook up the tow rope to my truck. See you out on the lake." Uncle Stanley slammed out the front door.

"Roger, my captain. Come on, Robyn; help me get the gang together. Out to our adventure... mom, sure you don't want to join us?" I gave mom another hug, noting once again her sad eyes. But she still was stunning with her perfect styled blond hair, pearl white skin, Hollywood makeup and her trademark deep, red lipstick. And with her Christmas reindeer sweater and black ski pants, I had to admit she was beautiful and would soon attract the next boyfriend to replace the previous Mr. Jerk. Of course there was the small problem of her tummy pooching out several inches. Yup. Five months or so and Christy and I would have a new brother or sister. What was mom going to do?

"Justin, can Sarah and I go out on the lake with you guys?" Christy asked, tugging on my arm.

"Why of course. Maybe Stan can tow us together in the saucer sled, but not too fast. We'll ask him. Come on."

Our burgeoning group pushed past the kitchen door, through the porch area and out the back door into the yard. The sun was setting over the tops of the pine trees and I realized we only had a couple hours of daylight left for our adventure. I held Christy and Sarah's hands and glanced over at Robyn and Marlene herding their younger brother and Stan's kids towards the frozen lakeshore. The snow crunched beneath our feet and our breath billowed out in cotton-white clouds into the crisp, winter afternoon. Stan eased his pickup truck down the gravel road and out onto the frozen surface of the lake. I still had reservations about him towing the kids behind his truck across the lake. I hoped he didn't have too many holiday beers and wouldn't get all crazy driving out there.

"So, who is going to go first?" Robyn announced as we congregated on the frozen lake. Some of the smaller kids were already shivering.

"I'll go," Marlene said. "And I'll perform on the skis as long as Uncle Stanley promises to keep it under one-hundred miles per hour." She glanced over at Stan.

I was surprised. *Quiet, always stay-in-the-background Marlene volunteered to be first?*

"Don't worry, Marlene. I promised your dad I would take it easy," Stan replied.

I looked over at Robyn and she shrugged her shoulders, indicating it was all right by her.

Marlene stepped onto the long, cross-county skis, strapped her boots in, and lined herself up behind the truck. Marlene tightened her stocking cap and scarf and bent down to lock both hands onto the wooden tow handle and said she was ready to go.

All the kids started jumping up and down and cheering.

Stan climbed into his truck, started the engine and pulled forward until the tow rope was stretched tight. His studded snow tires chewed into the three inches of fresh powder and then stopped.

"You ready, Marlene?" Stanley yelled out his driver's side window. Then he eased into first gear, while Marlene bent her knees and leaned forward. We watched him pick up speed, his tires spitting snow into the air, gaining traction on the lake's surface. He angled towards the center of the lake and the distant shoreline, faster now as Marlene slalomed behind his pickup. They reached the end of the first lake and Stanley began turning in a wide circle, whipping Marlene over the snow surface at twice the truck's speed. We watched her hang on, stay upright and then, with Stan, head back to our location. On approaching us, Stan slowed down and made a turn to drive parallel to the lake shore. Marlene released the tow rope handle and coasted to the bank next to the screaming cousins.

"Not bad, for a beginner," I yelled at her.

"Okay, Justin, it's your turn," Stan shouted out his window. He pointed his truck back towards the open lake.

"When can I go?" Christy asked.

"Next time, little prissy, missy. We'll go in the saucer sled. Meantime, I need to try these new skis."

Robyn flashed me a two thumbs up sign and Marlene called out how much fun it was while I positioned my boots onto the skis and latched them into position.

I grabbed the tow rope handle as Stan geared his truck forward.

The skis glided through the snow like a hot knife through butter. I tightened my grip on the tow handle, remembering to bend my knees, lean forward and stay focused and balanced at all times. Stan's tires on occasion lost traction and spun, kicking up clumps of powdered snow into the air and into my face. The skis made a hissing sound as we picked up speed, flying across the lake's surface, towards the end of the lake.

"Come on, Stan, slow down," I bellowed into the wind as he now arched into his wide circle approaching the shoreline. I braced myself for an increase in velocity as centrifugal forces spun me around the outside of our circle. He picked up speed now, even before I was out of the circle turn. My god, it felt we were going fifty miles an hour. His tires were spewing up snow into the air and my face. My vision became obscured as he continued to rocket over the surface of the lake towards our beginning point. I knew he was trying to dump me over and at this speed, if I fell down, I would tumble across the snow and break several bones. I prayed to the angels and held on. I was thankful when he soon slowed down, and shook the snow loose from my face and heard the screaming cousins cheering me on. I let go of the tow rope and coasted into the embankment. Wow! What a rush. Thank you, angels, for saving me once again.

"My turn, my turn!" Sarah yelled as all the kids and Robyn rushed over to me.

"You okay, Justin? It looked like he ramped up the Gs out there on the turnaround." Robyn put her arm around my shoulder.

"Yup. Got a little hairy on that outside turn, but I'm all right."

"Okay, give Justin a rest. Sarah, I will take you out on the saucer sled and then Justin can take Christy and we'll all take turns until everyone gets at least one ride and we'll see how much time we have left before it gets dark."

I helped secure the tow rope to the front handle of the saucer sled as Robyn and Sarah climbed inside. It was a large, round sled with plenty of room for two.

Stan edged forward and they were off towards the middle of the lake.

Everything went well after that. I took Christy out for a saucer ride and then Robyn and I alternated back and forth taking the rest of the kids out for their turns. Robyn tested the skis out once and I noticed how Stan pulled her and Marlene much slower than when he pulled me. I couldn't help wondering if he was still in revenge mode for Randy's murder and Gusta being sent to prison. Asshole. Uncle Stan was the one who should have gone to prison for his part in Randy's death. Then I remembered it was Christmas and needed to put away negative thoughts.

"Okay kids. That's it," Robyn said. "It's getting dark and time to go in for dinner. We have to get ready 'cause I hear rumors Santa Claus is flying around near our house and will visit us later tonight."

The cousins complained about not getting more sled rides and then began cheering about the impending arrival of Santa. We trudged back to the house as Stan threw the saucer sled and skis into the rear of his truck and drove up the hill to the back yard parking area.

"Get cleaned up, everyone. Dinner is ready and Papa is starved," Grams announced.

The kids lined up at the kitchen and bathroom sinks, washed their hands and seated themselves around the table in the family room. All the adults and older kids sat down at the table in the living room.

Aunt Pauline had arrived with Steven, her boyfriend from college.

I gave her a hug, noting her heavy strawberry-scented perfume, her glistening light brown long hair, brown eyes, tanned skin and perfect figure. Lucky Steve. I glanced around, counting almost twenty hungry, noisy people at the two tables. How did Grandma handle it all?

"I would like to have a blessing on the food before we begin," Grams said. "Pauline, dear daughter, would you say that prayer for us?"

Pauline offered a blessing and prayer and we started the feast.

I loaded up my plate with a couple pieces of roasted turkey, a slice of ham, mashed potatoes and gravy, carrot-raisin salad, corn-on-the-cob and a fresh biscuit. Across the table I noticed Mom wink at me and smiled. I was so relieved she was not getting drunk and seemed mellowed out this Christmas, as opposed to last year. I glanced over at the kids' table and noted Christy eating and giggling with Sarah, happy for her spending time with her favorite cousin.

Robyn, next to me, commented on how delicious the meal was, as usual. Everyone was talking, telling stories and eating. *This is the way family get-togethers should be. But I miss Audrey. Maybe next year.*

Soon, dinner was completed and Grams brought out her special, fresh strawberry-and-rhubarb pie, stacked high with whipped cream. I was so stuffed but I knew I had to eat Gram's favorite pie. After the dessert, the kids played games in the family room and coffee was served at our table. Aunt Pauline slipped over to the piano and began to play Christmas songs.

For the next hour or so, a bunch of us crowded around the piano, singing our favorite Christmas hymns and Santa Claus songs. I pulled Mom over next to me and we sang harmony on one of the songs. It was a memorable experience.

"Okay kids," Grandpa announced. "It is now nine o'clock and someone called and said they saw Santa Claus visiting some homes over at Parker Ranch on his way to our house. Time for everyone to hide in the back bedroom 'til he gets here?"

Christy, Sarah and all the younger cousins screamed in excitement, crowding into the back bedroom. Uncle Stan whispered he was going out on the roof just as Uncle Hal, dressed up as Santa, waddled from the guest bedroom into the front room. Everyone roared in laughter and cheered their approval. We heard Stan making thumping and scratching noises on the roof. Santa made himself comfortable in a large, overstuffed chair and the kids were let in from the bedroom to meet our guest.

Christy squealed in delight when spotting Santa and jumped in his lap. She was such a shy wallflower. The rest of the cousins were jumping up and down with unbridled enthusiasm. Aunt Pauline calmed everyone, assuring each would get their turn sitting in Santa's lap and telling him their Christmas wishes. Mom asked if she could have a turn also, and Santa replied, "Of course," and everyone laughed. It was fun watching all the kids take their turn on uncle Hal's lap as he listened to their wishes and gave each a candy cane. For a crusty old businessman, I had to admire uncle Hal. He was doing a great job.

"Ho, ho, ho. I must leave for the next home, where more children are waiting for dear ol' Santa. But before I go, I need one of you to help me light my pipe as a farewell gesture. Who would like to do that?" He pulled out a corn-cob pipe from his pocket, held it in place in his mouth with his red, woolen fuzzy mittens and offered a small match box to the children. Everyone stood in silence until Christy stepped forward.

"I will do it. I'll help Santa." She took the box of matches, pulled one out and struck it on the side of the box. Next she placed the box on the table and tilted the burning match head towards the pipe. She held it in place as Santa inhaled the small flame, igniting the tobacco inside the pipe. He inhaled again and blew out small puffs of smoke. Everyone cheered. Then Christy dropped the burning match. It tumbled from her hand, glancing off one of the red fuzzy mittens, igniting it like a stand of dry pine branches. All the kids started screaming as Santa tried to pat out the flames. I didn't know whether to start screaming with all the kids or laugh at this incredulous spectacle of Santa on fire. As usual, Grams kept her cool and tossed a large glass of water onto the burning glove, splashing Santa's beard and face. The fire was out and everyone, except Christy, was laughing along with Santa. I went over to give her a hug and assure her it was an accident and not to worry.

"Well, that's one for the history books. Rudolph, make a note of this crazy happening in our Christmas journal. Rudolph, where are you? Darn reindeer, never around when you need him. And, my little match girl, Santa is just fine."

"I didn't hurt you, did I Santa?" Christy was close to tears. Mom was hugging her.

"Of course not, no biggie. We have worse accidents at the toy factory in the North Pole all the time. Think nothing of it. But duty calls and I must be on my way. Merry Christmas to all and to all a good night." He stood up and waddled to the front door, waving good-by, and walked outside, calling for Rudolph.

"Merry Christmas, Santa," the kids shouted back. The door closed and everyone could hear Santa shouting some final instructions to Rudolph and the other reindeer.

"Okay, children. Santa left lots of gifts in the family room and it's time to open them," Grams said. Everyone crowded into the living room, seating themselves around the nine-foot tall Christmas pine tree, decked out in twinkling lights, tinsel and handmade ornaments. There were hundreds of wrapped gifts at the base of the tree.

"Now, everyone, behave and don't get rowdy," Aunt Pauline said. "Steve and I will hand out the gifts. Some of them are from Santa and some are from family members. If you get a gift from a family member, please say thank you to them."

I sat down on the family room steps next to Robyn and Marlene, watching Aunt Pauline and Steve hand out the gifts. Grams said not to worry about the wrapping paper, just toss it into the corner and it would go into the Ben Franklin stove later.

Soon, there was a flurry of wrapping paper tossed everywhere as dozens of presents were distributed and unwrapped. I looked over at mom helping Christy unwrap a large doll house complete with miniature furniture. Mom opened up my gift of a red and green sparkly Christmas bracelet and smiled at me from across the room. Robyn showed me her latest gold necklace from her parents. I thought about the gold necklace with a heart pendant I had sent Audrey and hoped she liked it. She had sent me a special photo of her in a beautiful Christmas frame. I wished this holiday spirit could go on forever.

"And what do we have planned for Christmas day tomorrow?" Robyn asked.

"We'll see how good you are on the ski jump hill," I replied. "Especially since I have doubled the size of the jump bump. My red Ryder sled is oiled up and ready to go. You will be faced with the ultimate downhill challenge of your life. Hope you can handle it, my fair maiden. We will also try out Aunt Pauline's new cat-and-mouse chase game on the ice.

"Justin, I can handle anything you've got planned. And by the way, tomorrow we call Eric and Audrey and start putting together our Easter break activity…going on our boat trip picnic, up the lake."

"As usual, your wish is my command. Tomorrow, we finalize our giant fish hunting expedition and decide which new harpoon gun and net we will take along."

"No, this is not a fish hunting expedition. We did that last summer and I don't want that monster fish tipping over our boat like he almost did the last time. We will stay out of his way and this will be a romantic lake cruise and wonderful picnic. Promise me, Justin." She flashed her unique smile and reached over, grabbing my ribs, tickling me. I could see Mom watching us with a peaceful look on her face.

CHAPTER 19

Barbara opened the overnight bag and pulled out the bloody garments, examining them one by one, and placing them back into the bag. With the angle iron, she lifted up the top burner plate of the small Ben Franklin stove and held a red-stained tee shirt above the flames.

"You sure you want to do this?" her mother asked. She reached over to give her daughter, who was now sobbing, a reassuring hug. Barbara dropped the shirt into the flames. "Mom, it's better this way. I didn't want to bury them in the dirt or have the funeral director dump them in the trash."

She reached back into the overnight bag and pulled out a pair of blood-soaked socks, held them over the opening and then let them fall into the flames. Next, she pulled out a pair of jockey shorts and a flannel shirt, both red-stained, and discarded them in the fire. She jabbed a metal stoker into the flames, pushing the smoldering clothing down into the hot belly of the stove. The smell of cooking blood and a hint of burning flesh filled the room. Then, she angled a pair of bloody blue jeans into the flames followed by a windbreaker jacket.

The last item was a baseball cap with a deer antler logo stitched on the front. She stared at it an extra moment before tossing it into the flames.

"Why are you burning all those clothes? Isn't that Dad's stuff?"

Barbara and her mother glanced over to the doorway of the bedroom, startled to see Justin and Christy standing there, watching them. "What are you doing, burning up dad's jacket and hat?" Justin screamed. "Stop it! Stop IT!" He ran over to the stove and attempted to reach in and retrieve the smoldering hat, beginning to cry.

"Shush, shush. It's better this way, Justin." Barbara grabbed his hand, pulling him away from the hot stove. "Your dad would not want bad memories of his bloody clothes hanging 'round, reminding us...."

"No, no. It's Dad's and I want to keep all of it. Stop it. Stop it!" Justin and Christy fell sobbing into arms of their mother with Grams standing nearby. The fire continued to eat away at the blood-soaked jacket and cap. Barbara fought back a flood of new tears, watching the dancing, mocking flames finish their task.

*

"And this present is for Barb, from Santa," Pauline smiled at her. Unwrapping the gift, Barbara glanced over at Justin laughing with his cousins while opening their Christmas presents. Christy came running to her open arms and snuggled up on her lap while rubbing Barbara's stomach area. "When is my little sister going to be born, Mommy?"

"Well, we don't know for sure if it will be a girl. We can only hope. But the baby will arrive the first week in May or thereabouts. Are you excited?"

"Yes, I am. I want a baby sister to play with 'cause Justin is too busy with his girlfriend. When are we gonna move down to the Cities with you and Kyle?"

"Probably the start of next summer, June maybe But only with me, not Kyle. I'm getting a new apartment near Jordan Park and the lake. You and Justin will love it there. You'll make new friends and help mommy with your new sister."

"Kyle is gone?"

"Yes my sweet, curious little daughter. He decided to move away."

"I'm glad. He had mean eyes and big, ugly hands."

"Let's talk about Christmas. I think I see another gift coming your way."

Pauline appeared and placed a large package into the waiting arms of Christy and winked at Barbara. "You doing OK, sis? Get anything for you?"

"I'm fine, Pauline. Thank you."

Christy tore into the wrapping paper of her latest gift. Barbara glanced over at one of the grandchildren setting up a small circular track with a key wind-up train beginning its circular trip. Chug, chug sounds came from the engine as puffs of white smoke belched from the tiny smokestack. She watched the train go 'round and 'round and 'round the track…and remembered.

*

"All aboard. All aboard." Barbara climbed onto the steps leading to the main passenger car, turned and waved good-bye to Mom, Dad, her two sisters and Justin and Christy. She entered the train and walked into the seating area of the main club car as the engine chugging sounds echoed around her.

"Welcome aboard, ma'am," the conductor said. "The transport car is ready now and you are welcome to come on back and check, make sure everything suits you."

She followed the conductor back to the transport car.

As she stood at the entrance, her eyes adjusted to the dim light from one faint bulb hanging from the ceiling, entangled in dust and old spider webs. She noticed a dead fly trapped inside the spider webs. There were no windows. The slight odor of formaldehyde lingered in the dank interior. She glanced around and noted three wooden containers in the boxcar. "Here is his coffin, all secured with an American flag attached to it, like your dad instructed us. You're welcome to come back here anytime and sit next to him. I got a nice dining club chair for you to sit in. Make it a little more comfy for you."

"Thank you so much, conductor, your name again is... sorry, I don't remember."

"Conductor Johnson. It's all right; don't fret if you can't remember. Just ask for Johnny."

"Can you tell me again, when will we be in Tooele, Utah?"

"About nineteen hours travel time, so be pulling in about eight a.m. tomorrow morning. Lunch and dinner, our treat from the train staff, don't worry about your budget, just show up and enjoy the meals. You take it easy on this trip and we'll be there 'fore you know it. But be careful; don't stay in this car too long. We keep it cool, ya know, for the preservation of the bodies and all. Take care, ma'am." The conductor left the car as Barbara sat down in the club chair and stared at the flag-draped coffin. She listened to the clacking, rumbling sounds of the train rolling down the tracks. *How ironic*, she thought. *A train similar to this one crashed into his car and killed my sweetheart and now another train is transporting his body to the family plot in Utah.* She stared in silence at the flag-draped coffin and began to cry.

"How could God be so cruel to take you away from me? What am I going to do with the kids? Oh God, oh God...help me get through this." She kissed her hand, touched it to the top of the coffin, arose from the chair, glanced at the other two coffins and left the transport car. A slight breeze swayed the dim light bulb, causing it to flicker on and off. The dead fly dislodged from its web encasement and fell to the floor of the rail car.

*

"Mommy, Mommy, look what Santa brought me," Christy screeched with delight, while showing Barbara some features of her new doll playhouse.

"Aren't you the lucky one. You must have been a good girl all year long, to get such a wonderful gift." Barbara glanced over at her son Justin, watching him laugh and joke with his cousins. He was growing up so fast, a teenager now. A pang of regret stabbed her heart as the past six years flashed by in her memories. It would be difficult taking him and Christy away from their loving grandparents and their close-by cousins, and family here at the resort, after all this time. But with this new baby and her dead-beat almost-husband gone, she couldn't manage by herself and would need their help...especially Justin's. *Got to talk with Harvey about getting more hours at the café. Need to remember to call Mrs. Rivers, set up another counseling session, get some stronger medicine. And tell her that I'll never go back to the State facility again.* A sudden memory flashed into her mind. She remembered being strapped down on that table with those electric shocks pulsating through her body. The pain, the arching of her back until it felt like it was going to break in half.

No more, never again. Whatever it took, with just her and the kids, she would make it this time. Forget all the worthless, bastard men and their empty promises.

"Mommy, can I go play with Sara and show her my new dollhouse?"

"Of course, Christy. I think she is trying to get your attention now." Barbara rubbed her tummy, feeling the slight movement of life. She put on a happy-face smile and joined the family singing, "Jingle Bells."

CHAPTER 20

I pulled on the starter rope, adjusted the choke on the ol' Johnson outboard and smiled to myself when the motor caught, emitting a growling, whirring noise, powering the prop blades under the water. I slid the accelerator bar forward and then back, alternating the speed, listening to the smooth engine sounds, satisfied the just-tuned up motor was in perfect running condition. Yes siree. This old dependable seven horse would take us up to the second lake and back, no problem. I checked the reserve gas tank by unscrewing the fill cap, sticking my finger into the opening, feeling the gasoline laced with motor oil almost spilling over the sides of the container. The oars were in the boat, along with the four life jackets, a couple of Gram's large woolen blankets and a cooler full of ice and sodas. My assignment was complete and Cruiser 2, Gramp's newest and largest boat, was ready to rock and roll. I stood up, stretching my arms towards the brilliant morning sun on this warm spring day. Thank God another frigid Minnesota winter had ended. The lake was melted and we would have perfect weather for our best picnic ever. I stepped out of the boat and onto the dock, glanced up and waved at the familiar Lincoln Towne Car pulling into the cabin parking area at the end of the gravel driveway. I ran up the embankment to greet my best friend in the entire world, Eric.

"Little brother, what an awesome day. You been praying to the Lake God again to make it so?" Eric jumped out of the front of the car and walked over to me, punching out a high-five.

I responded by slapping his hand with my full weight behind it.

"You know me. I do what I can to create the perfect ambience for our maidens. You hear anything from Robyn?"

"She called this morning when Gramps and I left. Said she and Audrey would arrive about eleven. Should be here any minute."

"Hello, Justin. Sighted any more monster fish lately?" Eric's granddad came around the front of the car.

"Hi, Mr. Hodson. No, I haven't been looking. With the cold water and all, the fish is probably up at the end of the second lake where most of the shallow inlets are, searching for his next bass dinner." I shook his hand and welcomed him to Pickerel Lake Resort.

"Okay boys, got your cooler here full of mama's homemade potato salad, sandwiches, and chips. It should last you through the day." He opened the trunk of his car and Eric set the cooler on the ground.

"I'll be heading back to Momma at her sister's place in PR. I'll be back around six tonight, Eric, to pick you up. See you then."

"Thanks again, Mr. Hodson," I called out to him. He waved back at us, got into the front of his fancy car, started the engine and pulled onto the gravel road leading to the highway. We watched him turn right onto number seventy-one, heard his horn honk twice and saw him speed around the bend of the road, out of sight. I turned to Eric, aware of a sudden uneasiness about the return of his granddad later in the day. Why was I feeling this way?

"Let's get this cooler into the boat. Our ladies will be here any moment. Is everything ready to go, Justin? You bringing along one of your high-powered weapons?"

"You think I should? Robyn gets nervous every time I bring a rifle."

"Know what? Not necessary. My gramps let me borrow his twenty-two, semi-automatic pistol and I have it wrapped in an old towel in my cooler, in secret, case we need it. Don't tell the girls…it would just get them freaked out."

Eric picked up his cooler and we strolled down the hill, onto the dock and loaded it into our new boat.

"Wow. Awesome boat. Your gramps bought it this year?"

"Yeah, it's the newest one. We made a little extra money from the tourists last summer, so he invested in our watercraft here. I promised him I would take care of it, so we need to be careful on the lake today."

"The girls will love this bigger, new boat. Don't worry…everything will be fine, since we are not fishing or hunting on this trip. So Justin, how was school this year? You write and call Audrey all the time?" We started up the embankment.

"School was Okay…especially bumping into my cousins every day. Audrey and I kept in touch. I guess the security thing with her dad is about over and they can come down to visit more often. But how about you, lover boy. You gonna marry

165

Robyn this summer or just get her pregnant?" I laughed, slapping Eric on the back.

He reached up, grabbed my arm and started to twist it behind my back. I pivoted around, bent down and swung my leg across his, knocking us both to the soft ground. Course he was still bigger and stronger than me, but I could tell he was surprised by my move. We wrestled around on the ground for a few moments then stood up and I adjusted my black glasses. He punched me in the shoulder.

"Well, defender knight. You're doing better, practicing that Gusta move I showed you. And I can tell by the strength in your arms, you have been doing your push-ups."

We walked up to the top of the hill with Eric outlining our day's activities. He was in charge again, but I didn't mind. I would be focusing all my attention on Audrey.

A series of car honks drew our attention towards the driveway. Uncle Hal's Cadillac turned the corner at the top of the gravel road and coasted down to us. I could see Robyn in the front seat, smiling and shouting something inside her car. Her dad slowed and crunched to a stop in their cad. Robyn threw open the passenger door, bolted from the car and hit the ground running to us, into Eric's open arms. I glanced up to see the back door open and Audrey stepping out, waving at me. My heart jumped in my chest. We raced towards each other, stopped for a brief moment, whispered a hi and then she grabbed me around the neck as I picked her up off the ground and swung her in a circle. I couldn't do that last year and again was grateful for the pushups. I stopped twirling. We were both laughing and then she tilted her head towards mine and we pressed our lips together in a deep, blissful kiss. We opened our mouths, continuing our embrace while the world began to spin. God, this was heaven.

"Justin, my strong knight. You have grown two inches taller and added all that extra muscle. For me?" she asked.

"Of course, everything is for you." We kissed again, took each other's hand and joined Eric and Robyn. I was in love again.

"Well, my dear. You aren't going to forget your favorite cousin now, are you?" Robyn came over, we both hugged and she kissed my cheek.

"Of course not. I did not want to interrupt your special moment with Eric."

Audrey stepped over and gave Eric a soft kiss on the lips. I was jealous…only for a second.

"Humph. Your flirting done so we can unload the car? Got to run back to town and pick up your mom for a shopping trip to PR. Not looking forward to that." Uncle Hal headed to the trunk of his car.

"Oh. Sorry, Daddy. Come on, guys. We got a cooler full of fried chicken, salad and dessert. "Eric and I helped Robyn unload the cooler and extra light jackets for the girls.

"Need to leave, Robyn. Now you kids take it easy out on the lake and be careful. I'll be back around six p.m. and you be ready to go. Don't make me wait on you."

Uncle Hal scowled a good-bye to Robyn and climbed into his Cadillac. He started the car, drove up the gravel road to the top of the hill, turned out on the highway and sped towards PR.

"Daylight is burning," Eric said. "Is everyone ready for our cool fish-hunting, picnic adventure?"

"No, bad boy, Eric. Justin promised me we are not hunting any giant fish today like we did last summer. This will be a quiet, romantic boat excursion and picnic lunch. And I brought my portable radio with us so we will have mood music at our banquet."

"Come on Robyn," I said. "Eric's letting his mouth flap away, out of control, as usual. We are not going fish hunting. Climb in, my damsels. Your water carriage awaits."

I reached for Audrey's hand, guiding her to the dock while Eric picked up the cooler and their extra jackets. We approached the edge of the dock and I held the boat steady as the girls maneuvered into the boat. Audrey wore a white, yellow-trimmed silk blouse and a light-yellow mini skirt riding just above her knees. I couldn't help but notice her slender, already tanned legs as her skirt brushed my face. She sat down on the cross plank near the stern of the boat where I would be controlling the motor. Robyn stepped in and sat near the bow of the boat, with a folded blanket on the plank, waiting for Eric. Both girls had their hair styled, darkened eyebrows and lashes and radiant-colored lipstick. Robyn had on a red-orange color and Audrey lips were bright pink. I hoped they had extra lipstick tubes because their current lip gloss would soon be rubbed off once we set up for our picnic.

I climbed into the boat and sat down next to Audrey, adjusting the Johnson while Eric placed the anchor into the keel hold and pushed the boat away from the dock. He jumped in at the last second as the bow of our Cruiser 2 pointed towards the open lake. I pulled on the starter rope and the engine caught in a low growling resonance as I turned the motor handle, directing our craft away from the dock, aiming at the middle of the lake. We were on our way. I glanced up to watch a red-winged blackbird follow us for a brief moment out onto the lake. He turned around and winged his way back to the shore, cawing out three times before landing on top of a pine tree. A shiver ran up my spine. Three quick caws from a blackbird always signaled danger to the other birds.

CHAPTER 21

"Let me captain our craft. Please, Justin. Dad never allows me to pilot our boat when we go fishing."

"Of course. It's all yours." Audrey slid over close to me, placed her hand on the Johnson steering arm and angled the boat closer to shore. A lake breeze whispered her blond tresses away from her face, shadowed by her new, butterfly-decorated sunbonnet. Her pink lipstick glistened in the sun rays reflecting off the mirrored lake surface. I reached over the side of the boat, dangling my fingers in the icy water, collecting a few drops that I flicked at her open blouse, onto the tops of her half-exposed breasts. She shrieked back at me, dipped her hand in the water and returned the splatter into my face. She pouted her moist lips and smacked-blew me a kiss.

I glanced forward to Eric and Robyn, envious of their cuddling posture at the keel of the boat. Eric mouthed something about keeping an eye on our crazy woman driver and I replied by dipping my hand into the lake and splashing water in his direction. He returned the favor and I ducked, calling for a truce.

Audrey asked for directions and I pointed out a lily pad-covered inlet at the end of the lake on the Southwest shore. This would be on the shore location opposite and away from the dark water lair of our monster fish. I did not want to tackle with our nemesis on this particular day. Today would be idyllic and devoted to peace and quiet, and love.

Audrey angled our boat towards the selected spot and adjusted the speed lever down a couple notches. I explained to her there was a clearing on top of the first hill sloping up from our intended lakeshore location. It was under some pine trees with a view of the entire lake, the perfect spot for our picnic.

The boat slowed in its approach to the cluster of lily pads when I looked down and caught a glimpse of a swirl of water cutting across our watery path. The inlet water was turning an uncharacteristic dark blue color. I called out to Eric to take a look at the spot I pointed to and give his opinion. He unwrapped his arms from around Robyn, stood up and scowled down at the blackened, blue lake water. Audrey glanced over at me with concern clouding her face. I asked her to shut the motor off so we could listen to the forest sounds as we coasted to the landing point.

She turned off the Johnson as Eric and I both stood up, listening for the welcoming from the birds and crickets. There was none. It was graveyard quiet. I looked down at the black water again, watching a swirl...building, returning, this time in a circular pattern around our boat. The swirl intensified beneath the surface of the lake, creating a whirlpool effect. The water trough deepened and our boat began to spin in a circle, following the whirlpool motion. Robyn screamed and Eric and I sat down, pulling our ladies close to us.

"What the hell is going on, Justin?" Eric screamed at me. "Is that damn fish back again getting all weird on us?"

"I have no idea. We're not even close to its hunting ground."

The spinning vortex deepened as our swirling boat picked up circular speed. I began to worry we would be capsized.

"No way. This is going to cease and desist now." Eric reached into his cooler, pulled out his loaded pistol, apologized to Robyn and told us to cover our ears. He pointed his weapon over the side of the boat and fired off three rounds into the main ripple, the swirling section of the water.

Robyn let out another scream and I pulled Audrey close to me and said a quick prayer.

The ripple effect in the water began to disappear. The circular vortex slowed down and then dissipated. The boat stopped its spinning motion, the lake's surface returned to being flat and calm and everything grew quiet once again.

"Listen," said Audrey.

I could hear it. A redwing blackbird was screeching from the top of a pine tree by the lakeshore. Then, several other birds joined in with their own melodic chorus.

Eric smiled, wrapped the gun in a towel and placed it in the bottom of the cooler, covered by the sandwiches.

"What was that all about?" asked Robyn. "This was supposed to be a quiet, peaceful activity for us. Was it that stupid fish again?" Robyn was close to tears as Eric encircled her in his arms.

"It's over, Robyn. Sorry for everything. We're safe now. Think it was some kind of territorial warning. Little brother, start the motor back up and get us to shore."

"Right on, captain." I pulled the starter rope and angled our chugging motor boat through the lily pad cluster, crunching the bow into the gravel shoreline.

"See, Justin? That fish is so dangerous," Audrey half-cried. "Dad told me his department is coming up here in a couple weeks with special netting equipment to capture that fish. Only then will Pickerel Lake be safe again."

"Sounds good to me. But did you mention to him, my love, that there are two fish?" I kissed the end of my index finger and touched the tip of her unique, model-like, ski-jump nose."

"I will tell him this weekend...when we get back. Promise."

"Forget Mr. Fish. He is gone. Let's unload this puppy and focus on the main event." Eric jumped out of the front of our boat, assisted Robyn to shore and pulled the anchor rope, lifting the bow up onto the gravel shore. I helped Audrey climb out and began handing the coolers and blankets to Eric on the shore.

"Is that one of your fishermen?" Eric asked, pointing out to the open lake.

I glanced up, spotting a large speedboat cruising into a full U-turn circle, about five hundred yards out from us. I noticed two men staring towards us, one with a pair of binoculars. They finished their turn and sped towards the other end of the lake.

"Nah, too early in the season for our tourists. Someone else who has their own cabin, trying out their new waterskiing craft."

Eric responded with a scowl on his face as we finished unloading the boat. I glanced out at the retreating high-speed craft disappearing from view and felt a quiver of uneasiness about our mystery visitors.

"We're burning daylight, private," Audrey quipped. "Get a move on, soldier, and assemble this camp."

"Yes sir. We hear and obey," I said in return. We all laughed, grabbed our gear and started up the hill.

CHAPTER 22

Only a short climb and we were over the crest of the hill, approaching the clearing. It was flat with an apron of pine needles covering the ground and a perfect view of the lake. Raspberry bushes nearby sprouted a few early, dark red berries.

We trudged over to our chosen spot and deposited the supplies on the ground. Robyn and Audrey wasted no time unfolding Gram's two extra-large blankets and smoothing them over the ground. Robyn dialed up her portable radio, filling the forest with one of our favorite rock n' roll songs.

"Who's hungry?" asked Robyn. "After all that excitement of shooting at a monster fish, and lugging all our stuff up the hill, everybody is probably starved. Sit down, brave knights; your maidens will serve you."

We positioned ourselves around the blankets as the girls opened the two coolers, handed out sodas and loaded our plates up with fried chicken, potato salad, chips and sandwiches. Everything looked almost as good as one of Gram's meals.

We sat around, enjoying a great lunch and singing along with the music. Eric and I started to review the fish-vortex incident when Robyn put her finger to Eric's lips and told him to please shush. She was right. Time to enjoy the moment.

We finished the meal and Audrey cut a big slice of black forest cake for each of us. I was stuffed, but forced myself to gobble down a piece since it was her secret recipe. We cleaned up, placing everything back into the coolers. Now it was time to relax. Audrey motioned me over to the edge of a blanket, sat, placed her folded jacket on her lap and told me to lie down with my head on her lap. Only too happy to comply, I lay on my back, looking up at the majestic pine trees soaring into the azure sky above us. Course I was visually drinking in Audrey's bedroom eyes and her brilliant pink-glossed sparkling lips.

She cupped a hand beneath my head, raised me up and brought her lips down on mine. Her mouth opened and she began dancing her tongue over the tip of my tongue.

I closed my eyes, savoring every second of the French kiss heaven. She cradled my head back down, smiled at me and began stroking my hair while humming along with a melody from the radio. I glanced over at Eric and Robyn, stretched out on the other blanket, kissing and rubbing their bodies against each other. Guess it was a good thing there were chaperons along on this hot picnic date. I closed my eyes, focused on Audrey's sensuous fingers gliding through my hair and dozed off.

"Let's go exploring," Audrey announced. "Wake up, my sleepyhead. You've been out for thirty minutes and Eric and Robyn need to come up for air."

I stretched my arms up in the air, placed my hands behind Audrey's blond ringlets, and while easing her face down to mine, pressed our lips together for one more long, delicious kiss.

"Okay, I'm ready. Eric, time for a walk on the wild side," I yelled over to him. Robyn and Eric struggled to their feet, adjusted their clothing and reentered the world of reality. Audrey led Robyn over to a nearby tree, pocket mirror, makeup brush and fresh lip gloss in hand. Eric gave me a high-five and asked what was next on the agenda. The girls returned, stored their beauty treasures back in a cooler, smoothed down the front of their blouses and skirts and announced they were now ready to greet any wild animals in the forest.

"Could be some brown bears, as a matter of fact," I replied. "Springtime, after a long Minnesota winter hibernation, they are on the prowl for some grub. But, we are on a narrow peninsula and not a lot of food out here. More back on the mainland in the thick brush area. I suggest we head up to the end of our peninsula and back...awesome view up there and about an hour round trip."

I led the way, holding Audrey's hand, towards a partial trail along the shoreline. Glancing back at Eric and Robyn, I noted she had convinced him to not take his pistol with him, but leave it wrapped up in the towel at the bottom of the sandwich cooler.

"It is so exhilarating to be out here with nature, listening to the birds sing, hiking with my best friends in the entire world," Audrey announced to the forest. "Justin, I missed you guys terribly when I had to leave in the middle of the night with my family. And I miss dear, sweet Randy too and wish he could be with us. Did they ever find the other persons involved in his murder?"

"No, not really. Eric and I made a trip to a club in the Cities, owned by a couple brothers Gusta implicated in Randy's death. We found some evidence, took pictures of it and turned the photos over to Sheriff Cooper in town. The sheriff said he was going to get search warrants and have the DA indict those creepo brothers as accessories to Randy's murder, but we haven't heard anything else. Probably nothing else will come of it."

"Sounds so dangerous. Those brothers don't know you and Eric are involved, uncovered this evidence against them, do they?"

"Nah. I'm sure the sheriff didn't say anything to them when he got the search warrants. I'm confident of that."

"Life is so difficult," Audrey said. "Will truth ever triumph…especially in this situation so close to you?"

"Don't know, don't know. At least we never gave up and for cousin Randy's sake and for his memory, we gave it our best effort."

We continued on the path towards the end of the peninsula. I looked back at Eric and Robyn, assured they were keeping up and not detouring off somewhere by themselves. And there it was: the tip of the peninsula, jutting out into the massive second lake. We all stood on a small sand dune, on top of a hill, overlooking a forever view of blue-green water stretching a couple miles across to the distant shores of Pickerel Lake Two. The sun was beginning its slow descent towards the horizon, indicating about three more hours left in our perfect day. A crane flew over us and skimmed to a landing near the shoreline. A loon echoed his unique warbling call across the bay to the left of us. I turned Audrey around to me, encircled my arms around her and we embraced in another long, blissful kiss.

She took both my hands in hers, turned her face away, for a moment, checked her emotions and her tears.

"I don't know where all this is leading, Justin, but I do know I am falling in love with you. Of course our parents tell us we are too young to understand what love is all about. But I know, with all we've been through together…the cabin adventure, the monster fish, Randy's death, me having to move, and being together today…all this has only made me more sure of my feelings for you."

"You know I feel the same way, Audrey. Sometimes I can't believe how lucky I am to have you in my life. It amazes me that you could love a poor resort boy like me. Afraid I don't bring much to the table except my love for you."

"Stop putting yourself down, Justin. You are a fascinating, kind-hearted person who knows how to treat a girl with respect. And I might add, always keep life exciting."

"And it will get even more exciting when your dad comes up later in the spring and tries to capture the monster fish. Is that true? Are you coming with him?"

"Not too clear what is going to happen at this point. Please don't tell anyone else about this and I will be sure to let you know when we leave. I will convince my dad to let me and my mom ride along and I'll see you then."

"Okay you two, we promised not to talk about the monster fish to keep this a positive trip," Robyn said.

"But I have to admit, this is a special day we will remember forever."

"I guess we should head back and have one more slice of Audrey's delicious cake before we return home," Eric said. "But before we leave, look at all these cool flat stones here on top of our sand dune. It's time for a rock-skipping contest."

He bent down and picked up several flat stones and handed one to each of us.

"These are the rules: The first contest will be to get the greatest number of skips per stone. I'll start, and demonstrate how an expert performs this amazing feat."

Eric stepped up to the edge of the hill, arched his arm back and then threw his grey, flattened rock across the surface of the lake. It skipped five times, sinking down over a hundred yards out from shore. Robyn went next and got four skips. I took my turn and also got four skips. Then Audrey stepped up to the mound, pointed both arms to the sky, assumed a straight silhouette position like a ballet dancer and spun around once, letting her stone fly across the lake surface. It skipped six times.

Everyone cheered and Eric gave her a high-five.

"I had a boyfriend, couple years ago, who was a discus thrower in school and taught me some special moves. You have met your match, Eric."

"Beginner's luck. Next contest is for distance. Your ballerina, discus moves will not help you with this next challenge." Eric picked up four more stones and let each of us choose our favorite. Robyn threw first.

Her stone zipped across the lake, skipping a couple times, ending up about fifty yards out. Then I gave it my best effort and mine soared about one hundred yards from the shore. Audrey was next and almost tied my distance. Finally, Eric stepped to the stone-thrower plate and with a larger, very flat rock, skipped that sucker out almost two hundred yards. Very impressive. We all gave him high-fives.

"Right. Brawn over brains wins again," I said. "And the wind picked up at the end of the contest and carried your stone extra distance."

"Yah-de-dada-da. Anytime, little brother."

I grasped Audrey's hand, leading the way to the trail and our blanket camp. The sun was on our backs and despite the waning light of late afternoon, it was still very warm. We could hear the robins and redwing blackbirds, with their competing chorus, jostling for bird territory. In the background, juniper bug and cricket sounds echoed through the forest as we made our way on the narrow lakeshore pathway. We ascended the last hill and wound past the final clump of shrubbery before entering our camp area. Then we saw them. Two men and a woman, standing next to the trail, watching us approach. I stole a quick glance back to Eric and he mouthed a 'no-problem' response. We slowed our pace approaching the visitors. I prayed everything would be okay.

CHAPTER 23

"Hi kids. How you all doing? We were out taking a stroll in the woods and happened upon your camp. Everything all right?" The bigger guy was over six feet tall, with a muscular frame beneath his suspendered jeans and red-and-green checkered flannel shirt. He had ominous dark eyes, a bulbous nose, yellow teeth, several days' beard growth and a baseball cap pulled down over his forehead. His friend was much smaller with a nondescript face, ragged jeans and a torn windbreaker jacket over a tee shirt. The woman wore tight jeans, a red blouse, with brown hair dangling over what might be called a pretty face that seemed somehow familiar.

Take-charge Eric stepped to the front of our group and we came to a stop behind him.

"We're just having a picnic and waiting for our parents to come pick us up…any moment now. You guys got a cabin around here?"

"Nah. We're just trying out our new water-ski boat. We have some friends up here we stay with. We were also on the look-out for some brown bear. We done got us a early-season, bear hunting license and the hardware to take care of the job. You seen any brown bear running around here today?" The big guy and his friend both pulled around to the front of them newer 30-30 rifles. It appeared they were hiding the weapons on our approach. Why? I wondered.

"Nope. Haven't seen anything except a few birds and lots of insects. Bears hardly ever roam around this peninsula...not much food for them. You might have more luck across the lake in the heavier brush and pine tree area," Eric replied.

"Yah, we thought about that. You say your parents coming to pick you up soon? They coming across the first lake by boat?" the big guy asked.

"Naw, they're fishing at the East bay inlet, here in the second lake. Coming by to pick us up any time now. It's been great talking with you, but we need to get our stuff ready to go at our camp 'cause our parents will be here any minute. Come on, guys." Eric waved us forward and we began moving past them towards our blankets.

"Yah, okay. Who's that nice Cruiser 2 belong to, anchored down the hill over there?" The big guy raised his rifle, pointing it towards us and then leveling it at our boat down the hill, at the lakeshore.

"Some of our friends left it there. They're exploring the other end of the peninsula," Eric said. "They're on their way back and we're gonna leave together."

"Oh, now you have friends here with you? How come you didn't mention them before? Know what, ass wipe, I think you are lying. There are no friends and that cruiser belongs to you and you are also lying about your parents coming to pick you up. I got it about right?" The big guy and his friend pointed their rifles at us while the girl flashed a weird smile. Audrey stepped closer to me, clutching my arm. I whispered to her to be calm and let Eric handle everything.

"Well, you are right. We did bring the cruiser but our parents are meeting us soon in their own boat and we're all heading back together."

"More lies. Homer, don't it all sound like a bunch of fucking nonsense to you?"

"Sure does, Jake. Almost like a…on-the-spot, made-up, fairy tale. And the food, you said we'd check on the food."

"Yur right on, Homer. Hey kids, we're awfully hungry. You don't mind sharing some of your grub with your neighbors now, do yah? While we wait on your parents. Ha, ha."

"Of course not," interjected Robyn. "We have plenty left over and you are welcome to it. Come on, guys." She grabbed Eric's hand and led the way as we followed her to our blankets and coolers. Our visitors trudged along behind us, pointing their rifles in our direction. Audrey glanced over at me with a dozen questions racing across her anguish-filled face.

"Here we are. Make yourself at home," said Robyn. "We have leftover chicken, some sandwiches and sodas…help yourself." She bent down, opened up the two coolers and stepped back next to Eric. Then I remembered the gun in the cooler.

"Thank you, don't mind if we do. Appreciate your Minnesota hospitality. Here, Darla, hang on to my piece while I check out the food." He handed his rifle to the girl and began rummaging through the two coolers retrieving sodas, chicken and the rest of the sandwiches. He handed the goodies out to his crew and they all sat down at the base of a couple large pine trees with their rifles laid across their laps. They proceeded to stuff their ugly, fat faces. Eric's gun remained, wrapped in a towel, in the bottom of the second cooler. He looked over at me and rolled his eyes.

"Relax, guys," Jake announced. "Have a seat on your blankets there. This lunch may be on you this time, but come visit our friend's cabin sometime and you can try some of our grub. So, all you kids live around here?"

I shoot a look over at Eric, expelling a deep breath and he got the message. Keep up the bullshitting.

"Yah, our grandparents and relatives have several cabins up here. We have lots of activities going on all the time and tonight we're even having a bar-b-que with tons of relatives showing up, any time now."

"Sounds wonderful, don't it, Darla?" Jake was finishing off his sandwich. "And what about Randy? Will Randy be at the family get together?" Jake grinned his yellow-stained toothy smile, stood up and pointed his rifle at us. Homer and Darla also got up, with Homer leveling his rifle at us and unlocking the safety. Darla smiled at us and when I glanced back at her, her eyes and faced changed, just for an instant, into that strange, almost non-human appearance. I glanced over at Eric and then I remembered. She was that weird-faced girl we saw on the street outside of the Nickelson brothers' strip club in the Cities last winter.

"Who is Randy?" Eric replied.

"You know Randy. Come on guys...the boy who committed suicide that you two claim was murdered. And now, you're trying to frame some honest friends of ours down in the Cities." Jake's words knifed into my heart. The picture of who

188

these guys were, and their possible intentions became crystal clear.

"You're wrong. Don't know what the hell you're talking about," said Eric. "You got the wrong people here."

"Don't think so. Darla, we talking to the right boys here? Didn't you say you saw them at the club, passed them on the street one day last winter as you were going to work? Isn't that what you said?"

"Yup. These are the two little creeps I saw walking away from the club," Darla said. Her voice had a weird rasp, almost a growl in it.

"That's what I thought you said. And you boys broke into our storage building, searching for fake evidence you turned over to Sheriff Cooper. Now he's come down with these search warrants, caused all kinds of problems for the brothers, who happen to be our kin. Seems we got these court dates coming up and the brothers are not too happy about all this. In fact, damn unhappy and disgusted with this mess you two have stirred up." Jake turned, coughed up some throat phlegm and spat it out at the base of the pine tree.

"Sheriff told us not enough evidence to pursue the case anymore and he was gonna close it out next week," Eric replied. Man, he was a great spontaneous liar.

"More lies, Homer. Nickelson brothers told us, according to paperwork, they have to appear in court twice, over the next three months. Don't sound like a case shutdown to me. And with that other worthless cousin of yours, Gusta, continuing to flap his mouth, doesn't look too good for the brothers."

"So what do you want us to do?" asked Eric.

"Really too late…nothing you can do now. But maybe you could do something in the future. Like if you are asked to

189

testify on any matter concerning ol'' Randy's death, you will suddenly develop amnesia and can't remember a thing. Sound like a plan to you, Homer?" Jake started laughing with Darla joining in with her raspy gargle.

"Okay, you got a deal," Eric said. "We were just playing around, you know, junior detectives and all. Once we tell the sheriff it was all a joke, he'll close the case."

"Sounds good to me, my man. But you know, the brothers want you to remember our little conversation today, have it burned into your memory. You know what I'm talking about here? We want to make sure you always remember our little meeting today and the promise you just made. So, why don't all of you stand up and promise one more time you will forget all this foolish Randy detective work. How 'bout we start this promise gig by having everyone take off their clothes."

I watched Audrey and Robyn's eyes fill with terror.

"What you talking about? What does that have to do with anything?" Eric said.

"Oh, that will have everything to do with everything. Right, Homer?"

"You're crazy, man. We'll do it, but not the girls," Eric said.

"Well then. This party is going to get really interesting," Jake replied. He handed his rifle to Darla. "Keep your gun on them."

He walked over to Robyn, walked behind her, grabbed her hair and forced her down on her knees, in front of him on the blanket. She started screaming. Eric moved to her side as Homer shoved the barrel of his rifle into Eric's stomach, forcing him to back off. Darla clicked off the safety of her rifle and pointed it at Audrey and me. Checkmate.

Jake continued to twist Robyn's hair in his left hand, with the other hand, unsnapped a leather sheath hanging on his belt and pulled out a long hunting knife, that he brought behind Robyn's neck. He held the blade out and in one quick cutting motion, sliced down through her blouse, separating it into two parts. Then he touched the point of the knife to her back, told her to remain still, let loose her hair, pulled her bra strap out and sliced it in two with his knife. Robyn screamed again. "Shut up, you bitch, or I'll slice your throat. That was only the beginning. Homer here has been carrying on ever since he laid eyes on you. You'd like to screw a nice young virgin, right, Homer? Let me cut off her cute little sundress and her panties and Homer, you can go to it." Homer laid down his rifle and walked over, unzipping his pants.

"Stop it. We got the picture," Eric shouted. "We'll all take off our clothes."

Jake stepped back and pushed Robyn to the ground, motioning Homer to back off.

"Now that's more like it. Be more cooperative and no one will get hurt."

Eric and I pulled off our tank tops and Audrey removed her blouse. Then we took off our jeans while Audrey unbuttoned and dropped her sun skirt. We stood there waiting and hoping it would be enough. Jake looked us over and grinned. Robyn was curled up in a fetus position on the blanket, sobbing. I stole a look at Eric and felt the hate emanating from his eyes. I knew he was wishing he had stuck his pistol in his pocket before leaving on our hike. "Okay, just fooling with yah. Put your dick back in your pants, Homer...maybe another time. Kiddies, don't have to get naked. But we got some rope here and we're gonna tie you up for a spell. Help your lady up off the ground there, sport."

Eric rushed over, knelt down on the blanket and comforted Robyn, taking her in his arms. He snatched up his tank top and slipped it over her head, covering her naked breasts.

"All right. Everyone stand up straight and put your hands behind your backs. Don't try anything stupid or we go back to plan A and let Homer have a good time with the lady here. Darla, bring over that rope we were going to use to tie up the bear."

We all stood there with our hands placed behind our backs. Audrey was fighting back tears and I realized our perfect day had turned into the worst nightmare of our lives. Hatred burned into my heart as I wished for a gun, a knife, anything to attack our visitors and rip out their throats, tear their guts apart. Feeling the rope tighten around my arms and wrists, I knew our situation was hopeless.

"Now, lay down on the blanket and we are going to tie your legs together also. Don't want you running home to momma, tattling on us. Ha, ha," laughed Jake.

We all complied and they tied our legs together. I pulled my legs slightly apart, for some reason, as low IQ Homer tied them together with no comment. I looked over at Audrey still battling the tears and mouthed a 'so sorry ' to her. She nodded her head at me and whispered back, "It's okay."

"Guys, we gonna leave you here now, comfy cozy, tied up on your blankets," said Jake. "It has been a pleasure. The brothers wanted us to do a lot more to you, for the warning, you know. But I think you got the message. I guess I have a soft spot for foolish kids like you. One last parting message from the brothers: Back off on your little detective pursuits about Randy's death or next time we meet, it will be much worse. And you, Eric, whatever your name is, you got a big lying mouth, which I don't much appreciate." He stepped over to Eric, lying on the blanket, pulled back a big black boot and slammed it into Eric's gut. Eric groaned and turned over on his side. If only I had his pistol at that moment, I would have emptied the chamber into Jake's asshole face.

"Got to mosey on, young folks. Thanks for the grub. Sleep tight tonight and don't let the bedbugs or bears bite. Ha, ha."

Our visitors backed away, chortling, with Jake orchestrating the laughter. They turned and trudged through the forest towards their anchored speed boat. Homer pointed his rifle into the air and fired off two 30-30 rounds, the sound crackling over our campsite. Moments later, we heard their motor boat fire up and the waves crashing as they sped away across the lake.

Robyn was fighting back more tears, Audrey had turned her head away from me and Eric was still recovering from the boot kick in the stomach. It was getting dark and I knew we were doomed.

CHAPTER 24

"Robyn, are the ropes hurting your arms or legs? Are you able to move at all?" Eric asked. "Sons of bitches. When we get out of this, gonna get some friends, go down to their club in the Cities and take out those bastards."

"Please, Eric, don't talk about revenge right now," Robyn said. "We need to somehow get untied and return home before dark or our parents will be worried sick. And we are running out of time."

"Robyn is right-on," I chimed in. "Audrey, can you move over towards me? Maybe I can work on untying the rope behind your back." I rolled over and surveyed a scene of three other teenagers, tied up, lying flat on our blankets. I turned towards Audrey and she struggled next to me. We put our backs to each other and I inserted my fingers in the ropes, pulling at the knots. No success.

"Stay where you are, Robyn, and I will maneuver close to you and work on the rope knots," Eric said. He also rolled over a couple times, placing himself back-to-back with Robyn and dug his fingernails into the knots of the rope.

"It's not working. The knots are too tight!" Eric shouted in desperation. "We need something sharp to cut through these ropes. Did anyone bring a knife in the coolers?"

"Only a little plastic knife to cut the cake. Don't think it would do much of a job on these thick, nylon ropes," Audrey offered.

"If I could only stand up, I could back up against a rough bark pine tree, slide the ropes up and down and wear through them."

"Sounds like a plan, Justin," said Eric. "But how you gonna stand up with your legs roped together? Not looking very encouraging, fellow campers."

"Any progress on my ropes?" asked Audrey.

"No, afraid not. Can't see what I'm doing and the cords are pulled too tight." I let my hands drop in exhaustion, rolled around, twisting my body until I was facing Audrey.

"I know you will never forgive me and Eric for getting us into this mess. But believe me, Audrey, we had no idea these creeps would come after us."

"I know that; don't worry about it, Justin. It's another chapter of a very interesting adventure with you and Eric. We need to concentrate on getting free and returning home soon so we don't have to explain all this to our parents."

My girl, my well-balanced and thoughtful lady, was correct again. I rolled over on my back, gazed up into the darkening sky and said a prayer to the angels to help us out.

"Little brother, maybe you can help me stand up and I can hobble over to a pine tree and work on rubbing through these ropes."

"Sounds like a plan. I'm on my way." I began rolling over to Eric when I stopped to listen, was that a snort I heard? I glanced up, noting a clump of raspberry bushes at the edge, rustling back and forth.

"What was that noise, Eric? Is it a squirrel or skunk over by the brush?" Robyn asked.

We all rolled sideways, positioning ourselves to face the unknown noise. Then that familiar odor wafted through the air, into my nostrils, filling me with terror. I knew that smell only too well. The raspberry bushes pulled apart and a brown, furry head with beady yellow eyes stared in our direction.

Robyn let out a scream, catching the attention of the large brown bear as he pushed through the brush, waddling toward us. In the middle of our camp, he stood up on his back haunches, clawing the air with his front paws, thrusting his nose up, searching for a scent. He stopped, peering down at our helpless roped forms in front of him. Then he dropped back down on all four legs and while snorting at the ground, lumbered towards us. Robyn began sniffling, fighting back tears.

"Don't anyone cry out or move or alarm him," Eric instructed. "He's looking for food scraps and will not consider us a meal."

The bear stopped just short of our blanket area, staring at us with what appeared to be curiosity. He shook his head a couple times, growled and then continued to venture into our immediate area.

Audrey closed her eyes as the bear came up to her, thrusting his snoot between her tied-up legs, then sliding up to her face. She pursed her lips tight, keeping her eyes closed while the bear explored her face with his moist snout.

Then he grew bored, turned his head away from Audrey and stepped over to me. I closed my eyes as I felt his puffing nose close to my face. Then he sneezed, depositing bear spit on me. He didn't seem to like my body odor and trudged over towards Eric and Robyn. Then he shot his nose into the air and rose up on his back haunches. He faced the two coolers, his long, pinkish tongue dangling from his mouth. The aroma of our leftover food drew him to the containers. I turned my head, watching him lumber over to our coolers.

He waddled over to the first cooler, stuck a paw on top of the closed lid and tipped it over, spilling everything onto the ground. A couple bagged sandwiches fell out followed by the plastic container with the leftover cake. He pawed at the sandwiches with his razor sharp claws, ripping the plastic bags apart. With his long tongue, he curled the sandwiches into his mouth. Then he slapped at the cake container, snapping it loose. He sampled some of the cake, snorted at it and moved on to the second cooler. He tipped it over, spilling out a can of soda. With his snout, he rolled the soda can along the ground, then grabbed it between his steel jaws and bit down. The cola can exploded in his mouth and splashed onto his face. He jumped back, dropping the can, growling while soda dripped from his fuzzy chin.

I looked over at Eric who was fighting back a laugh. If our situation wasn't so dangerous and pathetic, it would have been the perfect scenario for a belly laugh. Audrey whispered a shush and Eric got hold of himself. Robyn continued to remain very still, staring at the ground.

The bear came back to the first cooler and was beginning to act like he was bored. He stuck his paw inside the cooler, scraping his claws around for any remaining morsel, dragging out a few bags of chips. One more swipe of his paw and he pulled out the towel-wrapped revolver. The gun rolled out of the towel and bounced over the ground, landing not far in front of me. The bear pawed at the chips, broke open a bag, sampled a few and then stopped, looking back at us as if to say, "That's all you got?" He sniffed, snorted his nose, like he was clearing his plugged sinus cavities. He shook his head back and forth a couple times, started meandering towards us again and then stopped... listening to a distant forest sound. He snorted again, shook his head, and turned to disappear into the underbrush. Amazing. He was gone.

"Thank you, God, thank you!" Robyn words burst out in shouts.

"See. He only wanted to sample our picnic lunch," Eric said.

"I thought he was going to start snacking on my hair," giggled Audrey. "And Justin, he didn't approve of your body odor, sneezing all over you. You still have bear snot covering your face."

Everyone started laughing and I joined in. Like, how good it felt to laugh again when we were so close to death.

"Now what? We are back to square one. Any ideas, Eric?"

"Got a plan formulating in the ol" genius brain. Our bear friend may have provided the key to our escape."

"Don't follow you, my creative friend."

"The pistol. Here is my plan. I will roll over, pick up the gun with my partially free hands, release the safety and prepare to shoot it. You will roll over to my back, place your legs in front of the gun and stretch them out, pulling the ropes apart as much as possible, close to the barrel of the gun. I noticed your ropes are not as tight as ours and have more play in them. You and Audrey will help me line up the barrel of the gun aimed at the ropes, pointing between your legs, and I will fire, cutting the ropes in half, allowing you to free your legs. Then you can walk over to a pine tree and scratch loose the ropes that are tying your arms together."

"Eric, that is so dangerous!" scolded Audrey. "What if you don't aim straight and shoot Justin in the leg?"

"That's why you and Justin have to line up the gun. It looks like he has about two inches of space between his legs when he stretches the rope. Plenty of room for me to place a clean shot between the legs, cutting the rope."

"It will work. Come on, Audrey, help us do this," I urged her.

Eric rolled over to the pistol, turned his back towards it and with his free hands, picked it up off the ground. He maneuvered it around, clicking off the safety and cocking the chamber. I shuffled and rolled over to his back, placing my legs in front of the barrel of the gun. Audrey and Robyn rolled over, offering their second opinion on the alignment of the gun with the outstretched ropes.

"Point the barrel of the gun a little more towards the ground and a little more to your right," instructed Audrey. "Please be careful. Justin, are you OK about this?'

"Everything will be fine. I trust Eric." I watched him adjust the aim of the gun and looked down at the barrel pointing towards the ropes, parallel to my legs. It should work. Please God, make it work.

"Everything lined up perfect?" asked Eric.

"Let me look one more time," said Audrey. She moved closer to me, angled her head and line of sight down the barrel of the gun. "It appears to be correct. Justin, my love, you sure about this?"

"It's our only hope, Audrey. Blast away, Eric." I pulled the ropes apart with all my remaining strength and closed my eyes.

I heard the pistol go off, tensing up my legs, waiting for the result. My legs felt numb from the pressure of the tight ropes. The force of the bullet ripped into the ropes, jerked my legs together and a bolt of pain shot through my left calf. I opened my eyes and stared down at my legs, expecting to see a pool of blood and blown-away muscle tissue. Instead, several strands of rope were frayed out between my legs and thank God, no blood.

"How'd I do? Shall I fire off another round?"

"Please, Eric, no. A couple ropes are torn apart. Let me see if I can break loose." I pulled my legs apart, snapping a few more strands of frayed rope. I put my legs back together and then snapped them apart, again and again. There was still one rope holding my legs together.

"Looks like you'll have to fire off round number two."

"Oh no, not again," Audrey cried.

"It will be OK. Line me up again and we'll finish the job."

Eric cocked the gun and Audrey instructed him on his aim. He pulled the trigger one more time.

I watched the remaining rope split apart.

"Success, it worked! Put the gun away, Eric. My legs are free and it's time for a stroll to the nearest pine tree." Audrey and Robyn let out a cheer and Eric mumbled something about, 'Told you so.'

I struggled to my feet, babying my cramped leg muscles, and hobbled over to a large pine tree with extra rough bark and no lower branches. I turned around, backed up to the tree, flexed my knees up and down, rubbing the rope against the tree bark. It only took a couple minutes and the rope fiber began to tear. I pulled on the remaining loose ropes and I was free. I shouted hooray and ran over to Eric and untied him. Then, we ran over to the girls and untied them and they fell into our arms amidst laughter and a few tears.

"Okay, little brother. Our pet bear and your bravery saved us once again."

"Not me. Your brilliant idea and expert shooting did the trick."

"Please, our wonderful macho men. Let's get packed and into the boat. It's almost six-thirty and getting dark." Robyn studied her watch.

"Remember, ladies, this is our little secret. No need to tell our parents what went down here today," Eric reinstated.

We packed up the blankets and the coolers and hurried down the hill to our boat. I said a little prayer to the angels, thanking them for a visit from a hungry Minnesota brown bear.

We threw our belongings into the boat, climbed aboard and Eric pushed us off from the bank. I started the motor and we headed across the lake, as Audrey cuddled up to me under a blanket wrapped around us. I held her tight to me as I maneuvered the boat through the whitecaps.

CHAPTER 25

"Gusta, you have some visitors up front. Make it quick and get back to your job," the yard sergeant yelled at him from the front of the half-acre vegetable garden. Gusta propped the hoe up onto a small apple tree and shuffled his way out of the dusty garden patch. He waved over at Jake, who paused in his hoeing task and smiled back while giving him the middle finger. What a crock, slaving away in this farm boy's field when he ached to be out in the woods again, trapping, hunting and killing. Got to put up with it…another couple weeks and he'd be out of here.

Gusta marched up to the back door of the minimum security office, opened it and trudged past the desk of a guard on duty in the hallway.

"Where you off to, boy? It's only one o'clock, you can't be done with that half-acre yet."

"Nah, getting there. Mack told me I got some people in the visitor's area."

"Well, make it quick. Daylight's burning and warden wants that garden finished today."

Gusta continued to the front office, checked in at the desk with yet another guard and walked into the visitor's room, wondering who came to see him with no appointment.

"You got fifteen minutes, Gusta, make it quick."

Gusta glanced back at the desk guard, fuming over all these guards managing every minute of his life. How this place disgusted him. And now this low class, slave labor farm job he was reduced to working? He thought about Justin; how could that creep cousin of his love digging in the dirt? Whatta weirdo. Deal with it. At least this was better than being sent back to his old prison where half the population was waiting to gang rape him. And soon, he would be out of here and back with his pa and brother at their place on ol'' Pickerel Lake.

"Well, Gusta buddy, long time, no see. How's it hanging for you?" He glanced over as the Nickelson brothers shuffled across the room. Wendell extended his hand in greeting. Gusta ignored the handshake and scowled back at them.

"What the hell you guys doing here? I didn't ask you to visit and I don't need no trouble from you now."

"Keep your panties on, Gusta. We're not here to cause you any grief, seeing as you all are gonna get released in a couple weeks. Wouldn't mess that up for you, no way. But we came by for a friendly discussion about your future...once you're out of here."

They sat down at a round table, motioning for Gusta to pull up a chair. He hesitated for a moment, pulled over a side chair and dropped down into it.

"So why you here? The Randy deal is over. I served the time for all of us and you assholes got off scot-free."

"Not exactly. That's why we are here for this little visit." Wendell leaned in closer over the table and lowered his voice to a whisper while glancing back at the guard standing at the end of the room, watching them.

"You see, that cousin of yours, Justin, with his friends, is stirring up muddy waters relating to Randy's death, causing us a heap of trouble. They even broke into our club storage shed last winter, took some pictures and turned over some bogus evidence to Sheriff Cooper there in Park Rapids. Cooper got a search warrant, went through all our stuff at the club and filed some proceeding against us. We had to hire a lawyer and get ready to go to these court appearances. The problem ain't going away."

"So, what can I do about all this shit? I'm finishing my time and I'm out of here soon. Pay the bucks to your attorney and he'll make it all disappear."

"We're doing just that. And we had some of our kinsfolk throw a little scare into Justin and his friends at their picnic in the woods a while back. Our folk warned them to back off on their detective work or there would be hell to pay. We think that did the trick, but you never know about that cousin of yours and especially his bud, that Eric prick."

"So it's done. They'll back off their hunt-and-search crap and you can relax."

"Here is the new wrinkle. Kinfolk told us they overheard the kids in the woods talking about a giant fish-capturing expedition being led by Justin's girlfriend and her daddy. He's a government agent and gonna get the government involved. The daddy gonna try to catch that fish sometime end of next month and we want to be there. We got a proposal for you."

"What is it? I ain't getting in trouble with the law again."

"Listen up. You'll be getting out of here, next couple weeks, right before the daddy tries this fish-capture deal. Our kin said your cousin and his friend are gonna be there, involved in everything. We don't want them around 'cause we got plans of our own. So we're a thinking, you scout your cousin, find out the location where this government dickwad is gonna take the giant fish. You let us know that location, do a little distraction job to stop Justin and his buddy from getting involved in all this and we take it from there."

"I ain't killing anyone."

"Naw, no killing...just distraction. They'll be tracking this capture job, probably watching everything from their boat. You could cause a little boating accident, tell them it's a follow-up reminder from the Nickelson brothers and they'll finally get the message and quit meddling in all this, go home soaking wet, and everyone will be happy. Ha, ha."

"What do I get out of doing this?"

"My man Gusta...always lookin' out for ol' number one. I like that. We'll pay you, of course...one thousand dollars, for your time and trouble."

Gusta looked out one of the windows into the yard, past the front gate and freedom on the other side. Only a couple more weeks to go.

"I don't know...Pa could really use the money. And maybe, like you say, Justin and his bud could use a final reminder, a lesson. But I can't screw up one more time on the outside or the judge'll send me back to prison. And what if I don't want to do this?"

"Then you lose one thousand dollars and the accident could happen, instead, to your pa or your retarded brother." Wendell stared at him while his brother Steve sneered from across the table. Gusta clenched his fists together, stood up and shuffled over to the front windows. He stared unseeing in silence.

"Let me think about it. I'll give you a phone call the day I leave this hellhole." He continued to stare outside, not looking back at the brothers. Wendell and Steve rose from their chairs at the table, scuffed them back in place and approached Gusta. Wendell placed his hand on Gusta's shoulder.

"Think hard about this, partner in crime. We make your cousin and his friend go away, capture that giant fish and everything will turn out, hunky dory. And if you don't help us and the boys cause problems and we don't get that fish...well, don't want to think about it. Now you best get back to work there in your garden...vegetables waiting on yah. Ha, ha." The brothers turned and strolled out the front entrance door.

Gusta clenched his fists again, turned and ambled towards the guard at the back of the visitor's room. All he could think about was being free again and hunting down his prey, in the woods, armed with several choice guns and knives. But now, it was all about self-control over his temper and waiting for the right opportunity. He could sure use that thousand dollars, but didn't know if he was up to creating a boat accident and injuring Justin. Maybe instead, he needed to cause the Nickelson Brothers to have an accident in the woods on their next deer hunting trip. Yes, he could arrange that...no problem. Decisions, decisions.

CHAPTER 26

"Come on Eric. Be careful. Robert is going to spot us and we'll be toast."

"Don't worry. He is too occupied yelling at his assistant, getting ready for the main event."

"This is so cool. You think the fish will actually show up?"

"Don't know. But they have plenty of bait strung out over the water and after a long winter, Mr. Fish or Mr. Two Fishes, whatever, will be starving for red, bloody meat."

We both rebalanced ourselves in the boat, peering through the overhanging pine branches that were hiding us from the view of Robert and his assistant just a few hundred yards away, across the inlet cove. We were at a perfect vantage point, watching and waiting for the giant fish to make its appearance. I thought back to Robyn and Audrey pleading to come along with us, but thank God, we talked them out of it and they were safe, waiting back at Gram's place.

"What is he doing now?" Eric asked. We both put our faces through the pine branch opening and watched Robert push a series of buttons on a control panel, mounted on a rectangular, metal box, imbedded into the sandy shore. Bellowing forth a clanging sound, a huge metal, mesh screen lifted out of the water, almost touching three dead birds, hanging from a wire, strung between two floating buoys.

Robert shouted an order at his assistant, pushed another button and the metal mesh screen opened at the top and collapsed back onto the lake surface. Another few minutes and it disappeared into the water. The partner shook his hand and they hiked back up the embankment towards their black pickup.

"See that? See their bait system?" Eric asked. "They stole our idea, with the dead birds hanging over the water, throats cut, dripping blood to attract the monster fish. Audrey must have told her dad how we got the fish pictures."

"So what, Eric? No big deal now. But I wonder if the fish will even show up. And will that steel mesh contraption really hold the fish captive? And does Robert know he could be dealing with two giant fish, not one?"

"Don't know. But it will be interesting to sit here, nice and comfy, and see what happens. Let's have a snack." Eric opened our cooler, handed me a couple sandwiches and sodas and closed it up again, babbling on about the impending event. We ate our lunch and watched Robert and his assistant conversing next to their vehicle. The sun was beating down on us and it was getting hot. I checked my watch and noted a couple more hours from now and Eric's granddad and the girls would be showing up here at the cove. I wondered if the fish would really make their appearance by then.

"Eric, what are we gonna do about that court date next month when Sheriff Cooper wants us to testify? Remember what the Nickelson brothers' friends told us in our encounter with them in the woods?"

"Yeah, I know. Been thinking about that. My gramps said we should not testify in person, but just give a signed deposition for general evidence. Let Gusta testify if he wants, but not us. I worry about that threat from those creeps. If it were just us, no problem. But I don't want to get Robyn and Audrey into any more trouble."

"Sounds like a plan to me. But what if the brothers get pissed off at the trial?"

"Tough titty, Justin. We can't live in fear for the rest of our lives. And it's not over yet. My gramps has some close friends in the police department in the Cities and there is a little surprise brewing for the Nickelson brothers and their Kitty Club. Those assholes will still get their payback for what they did to us…especially to Robyn."

"What the hell, Eric! Did you see that?" I gobbled down the last remains of my sandwich and pointed out towards the bait area of the lake, only a few hundred yards away. One of the bait birds was missing from the overhead wire. Robert and his assistant were running down the embankment towards the metal control box.

"What happened? What'd you see, Justin?"

"I saw a huge splash in the water, didn't see the fish. But now a bird is gone." Eric pushed his face through the pine branches for a better view. Then I noticed Robert's assistant, looking in our direction through a set of binoculars. "Uh oh. Hope we haven't been spotted, Eric." The assistant handed the binoculars to Robert.

"What the hell you boys doing over there?" Robert shouted across the lake cove. "This is a government-secured operation and you are trespassing. Get your asses over here now." I gulped hard and glanced over at Eric.

"Come on Justin…jig's up. Let's go see what this is all about. Besides, I want to get a closer look at their net-control mechanism." We jumped out of the boat, pulled it up on shore and jogged over to Robert's location. I was not feeling good about this new development.

Robert came over to us.

"Boys, you just can't stay out of it, can you? You know I could lock you up for obstructing a government operation. But since my daughter adores you two, I'll let it go for now. You need to stay out of the way until my backup team arrives. And you'll have to sign some paperwork agreeing never to divulge any of this operation to anyone, ever, now or in the future. Agreed?"

"You're on, Robert… but since we did spot the fish the first time, along with Justin's cousin, Randy, we were curious. Ya know, he saw the fish and took the picture. We only wanted to witness the capture."

"Okay, okay. Please stay out of the way now and let us handle the operation. I called my backup crew and they will be arriving within the hour."

"Sir, the water is swirling beneath bait number two," the assistant announced. Everyone glanced out to the bait area and watched the giant fish lunge out of the water and rip the dead bird from the wire then splash back into the lake.

Robert called for his assistant to get ready.

I noted the gigantic fish had deep, wide stripes running the length of his body. Monster fish number two. Then it happened. Fish number two swam back up to the surface of the lake as fish number one burst out of the water and tore the last bird bait from the wire.

"I'll be damned. Two giant specimens!" Robert shouted. He slammed down a series of buttons on the control panel, shouting at his assistant to stand by for the backup mode. His metal mesh devices yawned open and crashed onto the surface of the lake. The water churned and foamed like a huge washing machine gone crazy. Robert pushed another button on the control panel and the metal screen devices rose above the surface of the lake with two huge fish thrashing around inside the clamshell enclosures.

"Gotcha...sons of bitches. We trapped ya!" Robert's assistant hollered while giving Robert a high-five.

I looked at Eric with my mouth open in disbelief. It seemed like a dream watching our two monster fish thrashing around in their steel cages, right in front of us. But for an instant, I was saddened when I realized our Pickerel Lake mystery would soon be gone forever.

"Nice catch, Mr. FBI man. But we'll take it from here."

My body jerked around at the announcement coming from the tree line. The Nickelson brothers walked in our direction, pointing 30-30 rifles at us.

CHAPTER 27

"Justin, do you know these guys? What is going on?" Robert asked. We raised our hands and stood to face our unwelcome intruders.

"Sure he knows us," Wendell said. "Been doing business together since last year, when cousin Randy met his untimely demise." Wendell and his brother Steve stood motionless, leveling their 30-30 rifles at us, exuding a menacing threat behind their dark eyes. I glanced over at Eric with a foreboding panic growing in the pit of my stomach.

"These are the Nickelson brothers from the Cities," I replied.

"That's right. Your wrongly accused brothers Wendell and Steve, at your service. Wrongly accused over the suicide death of cousin Randy and thanks to junior detectives Justin and Eric here, we are fighting off jail time over some trumped up murder charge by Sheriff Cooper. And it's all over those fish pictures that we paid good money for. Your boy Justin wasn't satisfied with the $500 he made on the deal. No, he wants more, more, more."

"What is he talking about, Justin? You sold him pictures of the secret giant fish here in Pickerel Lake?" Robert asked.

"Randy's original picture and ours of the giant fish that he ended up getting murdered over. And these are the creeps, along with Gusta, who killed my cousin Randy."

"I'd be careful of your accusations, little worm boy. We could sue you for slander or maybe even shoot all of you in self-defense when you tried to attack us. You know, a nice fantasy story made up about the unfortunate deaths of you four, here in the woods of Minnesota. Kind of like the story Justin and Eric made up about Randy's death."

"And the spent shell casings, the matching boot marks and all the other physical evidence Sheriff Cooper has...all made up also," Eric quipped.

"Here we go again, Steve. Like our friends told us about their run-in with you two and your girlfriends. You, Eric, have a big mouth. Best be careful what you say. It could get you in a heap of trouble."

"So, what do you want, Nickelson brothers?" Robert asked. "My backup crew, six more departmental officers, are on their way and will be arriving in minutes."

"Probably true, what you say about your reinforcements coming. But we won't be here too much longer. We only want to take what is rightfully ours...those two giant fish you conveniently caught for us, struggling in your steel mesh netting out there in the lake." Wendell pointed his rifle towards the fish, lying quietly now at the surface of the water, trapped inside the clamshell-shaped, steel mesh devices.

"You got a big enough pickup truck to haul them away?" Eric asked. I held back a smile as I shot a scowl over at my best friend.

"No, Mr. Smart Ass. We got a little bit better plan than that. Now, all of you mosey on over here, next to this control box, kneel down and put your hands behind your backs. My brother Steve has some rope and we're gonna tie the four of you up, nice and tight."

"Threatening an FBI officer will get you twenty years or more in a federal penitentiary," Robert said.

"Not really threatening you. Like I said earlier, if we were, we would've killed you by now. No, only a little preemptive warning, keeping you out of the way while we retrieve our property."

Wendell waved his rifle at us and we walked over next to the control box to kneel down on the sandy embankment. Steve approached us, adjusted his horn-rimmed glasses on his rat-like face and pulled out several lengths of rope from his backpack.

I felt the rope cut into my arms as he wound it tightly around me, securing it with several knots. The memory of our last encounter, in the woods with the girls, flooded back into my mind as I watched him tie up the others.

"I don't trust these smart asses, Steve. Use that extra rope you have left over and tie up their ankles also." Steve turned us over and bound our ankles together. "Nice and comfy, guys? You know, we could easily kill all of you, but we'll let that go, for now. We will reserve that option for the future if you continue to…what shall we call it, meddle in our affairs. But a warning to everyone and especially you, Mr. FBI man. Once we leave here today, you need to close your files on this monster fish case and get on with more important investigations. Need to let you know, we have many important friends in high places, even at high levels of your precious FBI department, who are very interested in your catch today. In fact, one of your supervisors works for us and our leaders. You have no idea who you are messing with here, Robert. It is beyond your wildest imagination. So, take all this as a gentle warning and close down this case."

"Maybe we should go ahead and shoot them and be done with it," Steve said. He looked nervous as he stepped back and pointed his rifle at us.

"Nah, I think everyone has got the message, loud and clear. And Robert will find out soon enough we mean business when he files that report with his supervisors."

"We'll see, we'll see," Robert replied. "But I'm curious, how you are going to transport over a thousand pounds of thrashing fish?"

"Ah, now that is the final rub. A mystery you will never solve because we are now going to apply the final coup de grace. Steve, the blindfolds, if you please."

Steve reached into his backpack, pulled out four black, thick cloth blindfolds and tied them over our eyes. We were all thrust into darkness.

"Now just relax, gang, and listen to the beautiful sounds of your favorite fish being transported to their new home," Wendell sneered.

It got real quiet then, except for some splashing noises emanating from the trapped fish, out in the inlet bay. I tried to wiggle my eyebrows to gain a small peek into the outside world, with no luck. Then, I heard the whirring noise.

I could tell it came from behind us, above the tree line. It sounded like a helicopter, but with no downward air flow blowing on us, I wasn't sure. The whirling sound moved past our location and stopped...hovering over the lake in front of us. Suddenly, the steel mesh traps began clanking violently together like they were being separated from the stanchion poles supporting them in the water. The fish inside were going crazy, gyrating around inside their steel mesh enclosures. We heard massive amounts of water raining down on the surface of the lake, while it sounded like the steel mesh cages were being pulled into the air. The metal clanking sounds continued for only a minute or so and then there was that intense whirring sound and it grew quiet.

The soft helicopter-like noise began again, grew louder and then seemed to move away, becoming distant and faint. Then there was silence. "Well, my FBI friends and pesky detectives, wish you could have witnessed that, but will leave it to your imagination. We need to exit, stage left, before your other FBI friends arrive. And Robert, remember our conversation and listen carefully to the instructions from your department supervisors. I'm sure you can write a believable summary on this case when you close the file, describing how the fish escaped and crashed back into the lake. And Justin and Eric, hope we have convinced you not to appear in court, but instead, drop all your detective pursuits. Would be in your best interests and better for your sweet ladies also. And tell Gusta, he better keep his mouth shut. We have prison friends and outside contacts ready to take him out, any time we choose. See you all on the flip side."

I jerked in surprise as several gunshots rang out next to us. "Come on, Steve. Put your rifle away and stop celebrating like that. Scaring the good folks here. I swear, what ya gonna do with this younger generation."

"OK, bossy, big brother." We heard their laughter fade as they trudged up the embankment and climbed into their truck. They started up their engine, backed onto the gravel of the embankment, gunned their engine, burned rubber on the highway and were gone.

"Justin. Eric. You boys doing okay?" Robert asked.

"We're fine," Eric replied. "Maybe we can maneuver over next to each other and loosen these knots."

I dug my heels into the sand and scooted over next to Eric. We put our backs against each other and he went to work on one of the knots. It proved fruitless. Then we heard a car engine rev up on the embankment hill above us. A door slammed and a scream penetrated the air as I listened to several people clamber down the hill.

"Eric, Justin…are you all right?" I recognized Robyn's high-pitched cry. Soon, the blindfolds were removed, we were untied and I fell into the arms of my Audrey.

Eric hugged Robyn while Eric's granddad talked with Robert and his assistant.

Audrey pulled me over to her dad and motioned Robyn and Eric to join us. We all hugged each other in a warm, supportive circle.

"Justin, what happened here and what is that contraption out in the lake?" Audrey asked.

"Oh yes. Well, the Nickelson brothers paid us a visit, stole our monster fish and gave us our final warning about the detective work."

"The fish are gone? How did they get them out of the water?"

Eric and I were about to review the incident when another vehicle stopped at the parking area above us. A half-dozen agents scrambled down the hillside, weapons drawn. Robert walked over to them, with his palms motioning downward, advising them it was all under control. He was soon in a spirited conversation with the supervisor of the new arrivals.

"Audrey, the Nickelson brothers surprised us, tied and blindfolded us and then stole our giant fish," I said, holding her close to me.

"How can that be? We didn't see any huge truck or vehicle transporting fish out of here."

"We were blindfolded, but heard some kind of whirring noise, like a helicopter. It sounded like the fish, trapped in the steel mesh cages, were lifted up, out of the lake and placed into the copter."

"Could a helicopter lift that much weight?" Robyn asked.

"Or maybe it wasn't a helicopter after all," Eric said. "We don't know; guess we'll never know for sure." I pulled Audrey close to me and we trekked down next to the lakeshore. Robyn and Eric followed us.

"And we need to stop our detective work, Audrey. We were threatened again, you and Robyn were also threatened, and it is not worth it."

"Probably right, little brother. We have given it our best, for Randy and for his memory, but it's time to hang it up. And Sheriff Cooper has enough evidence to proceed to a possible trial without us."

I glanced back at Audrey's dad, watching him shout and wave his arms at the supervisor of the team. It sounded like Robert was being told to shut down the case and he was vehemently disagreeing with the call. I pulled Audrey closer to me, turned her face towards mine and kissed her moist lips, noting a tear on her cheek. "Let it go, Justin. We have done all we can for Randy and his memory. And those super-size fish are now gone."

"You're probably right. Your family is going to move back here this summer and we can have a wonderful two months together before Christy and I have to leave for the Cities to live with Mom. She will need help with the new baby and all. The mystery fish no longer swim in Pickerel Lake and I guess we will never know what happened to them. But maybe we could do some follow-up detective work and find out how those fish were transported to their secret location."

Eric rolled his eyes at me as he started humming that tune from our favorite science fiction program. Reaching over, I punched him.

I then pulled Audrey back into my arms. We watched the sun disappear on the horizon, reflecting a final orange glow over the water. I felt a tinge of sadness realizing the two mystery fish from Pickerel Lake were gone forever and our detective work on Randy's murder was finished. But I also realized my love for Audrey was only beginning and this next summer, it would be strengthened with new adventures together. Now if Christy and I could convince Mom to relocate here to Park Rapids instead of moving us to the Cities...life would be perfect. But little did I know how confused and imperfect life would become over the summer months ahead.

ABOUT THE AUTHOR

Gary Blackburn is the author of two previous novels and credits mysterious and unique experiences of Minnesota lake resort life as a backdrop for this story. He is currently drafting the third installment of the Pickerel Lake Trilogy.